WORDS TH

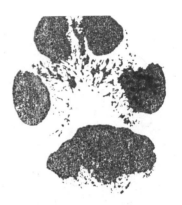

WORDS THE DOG KNOWS

A NOVEL

J.R. CARPENTER

Made in Montreal
by conundrum press

Some stories resemble real life, but this one is really fiction. These characters are all figments of the author's imagination and everything they say is make-believe. Except for the dogs. They're real, and they're telling the truth.

Edited by Andy Brown
Copyedited by Maya Merrick
Drawings by J. R. Carpenter

Library and Archives Canada Cataloguing in Publication

Carpenter, J. R
  Words the dog knows / J.R. Carpenter.

ISBN 978-1-894994-34-7

 I. Title.

PS8605.A7726W67 2008 C813'.6 C2008-905836-4

Dépot Legal, Bibliothèque nationale du Québec

Printed and bound in Canada
First Edition

CONUNDRUM PRESS
PO Box 55003, CSP Fairmount
Montreal, Quebec, H2T 3E2, Canada

conpress@ican.net
www.conundrumpress.com

conundrum press acknowledges the financial assistance of the Canada Council for the Arts toward our publishing program.

Canada Council   Conseil des Arts
for the Arts   du Canada

FOR STÉPHANE AND ISAAC

... the animals already know by instinct
we're not comfortably at home
in our translated world.

— Rilke

I am I because my little dog knows me.

— Gertrude Stein

Want to go for a walk?
If you were a dog, that would be a great opening line.

I never had a dog as a kid, which is surprising considering I grew up on a farm. We had every other kind of animal. Ninety head of cattle to keep the one bull busy. A pen of pigs to keep the one we'd eat company. A roost of free-range chickens run ragged by a mean white rooster. A hutch of show rabbits not good for much of anything. And thirty-five hives of honeybees — white wooden worlds unto themselves — each one run by a queen.

I had a housecat named Feather of the Fairies. Children below a certain age should not be granted the power to name. The barn had its own cats. They kept their own company, lived according to laws unknown to us, and came and went and fed and bred and killed in anonymity.

We had a horse named Red, even though he was brown. Red decided how fast or slow he'd go by the weight of his rider. The heavier you were the faster he went. My mother was barely five feet tall. But according to Red she weighed plenty. No sooner was she settled in the saddle than he was off and running. Splashing through the shallows of the cattle pond, up the slope to the rock wall, along its length to the northwest fence, and down again for a victory lap around the first pasture. Unable to rein in his canter, my mother did her best to avoid Red altogether.

My father was six-foot-two at least, skinny as a postcard sideways and solid as a cast-iron skillet. He rode Red to a froth. The two of them lived for round-up. There were other dairy farms nearby, much larger than ours. Most ran round-up with dogs. On our stretch of the Sloane Road alone there must have been fifteen herding and hunting dogs. And that's not counting over at the Doyle place where they kept a pack of sled dogs, twenty-four or more, chained all seasons. Their howled chorus blew our way on the same south-easterlies that made the power lines whine. It's not that I wanted a dog. It's that I was surrounded by something that was missing.

My parents were always busy. Work, work, work, that's all farm people ever do. I had chores too. I fed the chickens. I fed the rabbits. I brushed the horse. Sometimes I weeded the carrots. I wasn't allowed near the sweet peas. All I did was eat them. "Make yourself useful," my father said whenever I got underfoot. But then he'd disappear without any further instructions — out on the tractor somewhere or deep in the woodlot, alone with the chainsaw roar. "Make yourself scarce," my mother said when I got in her hair. She didn't have to tell me twice. I hated being inside: the hard corners of the house, the low ceilings, the small windows, the arbitrarily enforced order of pots and pans in the cupboards and cans and jars in the pantry. How tedious: towel-drying dishes that could just as well dry on their own. How senseless: folding laundry that we'd just unfold and use, then wash and dry and fold again. How boring: peeling potatoes, seeding squash, ending beans. I loved being outside: the wide open spaces, the hiding places, the trees to climb, the stream to wade across, the hay loft to hide in, the any-which-way of the wind. And then there were the edible seasons: the wild blueberries, strawberries, raspberries, blackberries, the wild mint and clover, the pale green sweet stems hidden inside some, but not all, of the tall grasses and the yellow heads of chamomile that grew at the edge of the hard-packed driveway dirt.

Feather of the Fairies was a decent cat, but all she did was sleep and shed fur that then needed sweeping. Occasionally she clawed at the couch, which was my fault. Once she climbed the livingroom curtains and got stuck up near the top. My father said, "Leave her up there." Until she learned her lesson, I guessed. My mother said, "Oh, my poor curtains."

Red, the brown horse, made a better friend by far. We went for long walks together. I rode bareback because I was only six and couldn't lift the saddle. Between the two of us it was hard to say who was in charge of whom. Once we got out of earshot there was no telling us what to do. I weighed nothing, so Red refused to move faster than a trot with me on him. Mostly we'd just saunter; sometimes through the cattle pond and up along the rock wall, sometimes down the Sloane Road to visit the neighbours.

Our nearest neighbours were the Vaughns. They lived in a trailer and there were a lot of them. The father's name was Jackie. He was an auto mechanic. "Jack of all trades," he said. "Doesn't know Jack," my father said. "Don't you repeat that," my mother warned me. There were five Vaughn kids. "And counting," my mother said. Four girls and a boy. The boy was closest to my age. His name was Jack too. And get this — Jack's favourite game was jacks. He got jacks for Christmas, jacks for his birthday. It started out as someone's idea of a joke but Jack went along with it. So did the rest of us. Onesies, Twosies, Threesies, Fours. In the summer we played jacks on the hood of the long white Ford parked out back, or in the scrappy yard in front of the trailer. If you walked barefoot on the Vaughn lawn, sooner or later you'd step on a lost metal star. In the rain and in the winter we hunkered down to play indoors on the concrete floor of Jackie's Auto-Body shop, or in between the built-in bunk beds in either of the trailer's tiny bedrooms, or out in the livingroom sprawled on the wall-to-wall carpet in front of the television.

The Vaughns had a television. We did not. We had floor-to-ceiling bookshelves all along the north wall of the livingroom. That's where the winter winds blew the fiercest. "Where did all these books come from?" first-time visitors to our house asked.

"Flea markets, mostly," my mother said.

"They're just there for insulation," my father said.

My parents spoke in very short sentences. They rarely ever spoke directly to each other. Between them they were so inarticulate that it was hard to believe they'd ever read anything. Yet books they had, and books they read, and books were just about the only thing they could ever agree on. Books saved them from talking to each other, saved them from socializing. We never went anywhere and rarely had visitors. My parents were from away, so there was no family to drop in on us, and our nearest neighbours knew enough to keep their distance.

There were Archie Digests at the Vaughn trailer, their pages soft as flannelette by the time all five kids got done reading them. There was little dispute over who was who: Jack was Archie. Because he was the only boy he got to be the best one. I was Veronica, because I had black hair. And every one of the Vaughn girls was a Betty.

The Vaughns had only one animal. Trixie was a smelly, shaggy, black-and-white mop of a dog not much bigger than Feather of the Fairies. Trixie ruled the Vaughn trailer. Doors opened and closed for her. She slept on couches and beds and ate whatever the Vaughns ate. Breakfast, lunch and dinnertime, Vaughn hands of all ages slipped scraps under the table, pretending not to feed her.

One day Trixie disappeared. For weeks various Vaughns passed by our place asking if we'd seen her. My mother was beet-red embarrassed. My father was indignant. "Don't look at me," he said. No more jacks with Jack. I made myself scarce. Through knotholes in the pine-board walls, through hot air burning up the woodstove pipes, I pieced together this story: Trixie had been caught trespassing on our property one too many times. "A rat with fur," my father called her. "Git," he'd said with his boot. "Go on," he'd said with his 12-gauge. If the Vaughns knew, I never knew. Not for certain. Even without their dog, between the Vaughns and us, they were the happier family.

Red and I still wandered down the Sloane Road toward the Vaughn trailer, but more often than not we'd turn before we got there, to walk up our logging road. Slow-going through ruts and mud and holes, Red sauntering, me ducking and dodging low-slung branches. The first quarter-mile was a cool, dark tunnel, through spruce scrub and sap-lined maple. Then the  road opened onto the north edge of the northwest pasture.

In the northeast corner of the northwest pasture sat the ruins of a house. Ruins of ruins, in fact, the vestiges of a modest stone foundation set so far back from the Sloane Road that there must have been a different road long ago. How else would the inhabitants have made their way into town? How long had it taken for that family to age and fade, for those wooden walls to warp and sag and rot into oblivion? Inexplicably ancient, these mysteries seemed to me.

Our own farmhouse was newly built. To hear my father tell it, he had cleared the land single-handed and split the logs himself at the water-powered sawmill down behind the Doyle place. It's possible. I've seen it, the sawmill I mean. In my mother's version of the story of how my father built our house, he drove a hard bargain for the board feet down at Caldwell Lumber. If that was the case then he got ripped off. Every board in every floor and wall and door in every room of our house had a knot or a crack or a flaw of some kind. If these walls could talk, their grammar would be weak, and their sentences stilted.

There was a kid named Isaac in my class at school who insisted that his dad had built our place, years ago, before my parents had arrived in Nova Scotia, before Isaac and I were born. Isaac was a skinny, runty, talks-too-much kid like me, so I was disinclined to believe him. He also claimed his dad had once played electric guitar in a rock-and-roll band. Now his dad was a trucker. He drove long haul with a big black Lab named Cinder in his cab, all the way to Montreal, Toronto, Windsor, Winnipeg, even. On his dad's every-other-weekend home, he and Isaac washed the rig together. This took the whole day. The rig took up the whole driveway. When his dad wasn't looking Isaac would shove Cinder away. The dog thought this was a game and came right back again. You only ever saw them in the same room together if Isaac's dad was in between them. Maybe Isaac wished he were Cinder, so he could go with his dad. Maybe he would have learned to love

Cinder more if his dad would have just stayed home.

Isaac's folks sent him to school in cowboy boots. The farm kids all wore sneakers. Most mornings, in the cloakroom before first bell, we'd trade. It wasn't like that, not what you're thinking. The most touching we ever did was me sliding my feet into his warm boots and him lacing his feet into my soft sneakers. Not every day, but many days, we made this trade. He preferred sneakers and I preferred boots. And it amused us that no one ever noticed. His socks had holes in them and mine didn't match. I had short, straight, black hair; his was long, curly, and blonde. I got in trouble for reading ahead in class, him for falling behind. We had nothing in common really, except for our shoe size. But we banded together on occasion. When the tadpoles in the swampy patch by the stream behind the school needed saving from some older kids, we were on the front lines. When sticks were needed for the field-day marshmallow roast, we found the longest, sharpest, greenest-wood ones. A band of two doesn't sound like much, but there were only six kids in our grade, only seventy-six kids in our school in total. When skinny talks-too-much Isaac and I banded together we were practically a gang.

I don't remember learning to read the way I don't remember learning to eat. My parents read so I read. My father took paperbacks out on the tractor with him, company on the long days of mowing and sowing, working the land one square foot at a time. He kept a shelf of favourites in the barn. Political things mostly. Thomas Moore's *Utopia*. Plato's *Republic*. Machiavelli. Orwell. Marx. My mother preferred stories. *The Illiad*. *The Odyssey*. Other kids got Beatrix Potter or Winnie-the-Pooh at bedtime. Not at our house. We started with Aesop's Fables and went directly on to the Greek myths. Jason and the Golden Fleece, the Labours of

Hercules, Theseus slaying the Minotaur. My advice is to not bring these subjects up in school, especially if there are only six kids in your grade, especially if you're not related to anyone. Even if you explain what myths are, and Greeks, chances are no one will believe you don't believe these stories to be true.

There was no chair in my bedroom. I fell off chairs. I didn't mean to. Once I spun right off the piano stool. I went flying and whacked my head on a table leg. All I got was a tiny little scab near my eyebrow. My father said not to pick it. My mother said if I did I'd get a scar. "What's the big deal about a scar?" I asked. My father said, "A scar never goes away." My mother said when I got older I'd regret having a scar on my face. At school I fell out of a chair and got a nosebleed. I didn't get a scar, but I got blood all over my shirt. I didn't think that was a big deal either, until I got home from school and found out that once you get blood on something you can't get it out. My mother said she'd paid good money for that shirt. My father said *he'd* paid good money for that shirt. Either way, it was ruined.

There was no chair in my bedroom, so my mother sat on the edge of my bed. Her weight sloped the narrow mattress toward her. I leaned away from her to keep from sliding toward her denim hip. She used to read me bedtime stories from picture books. I could fall asleep listening to those stories because the words came in a kind of rhythm. You didn't really have to listen to know what they were saying. When I started school my father told me, "Picture books are for babies." He told my mother, "Don't go filling the kid's head with nonsense." But my mother insisted, "Bedtime stories are important." My father said, "You might as well tell the kid

a good one then, like the one about the fall of the Roman Empire."
I thought the Roman Empire was something he was making up,
but it turned out to be a real thing. My mother started telling me a
bit of the story of the Roman Empire every night before bed. My
father couldn't argue with that, because it was his idea, but he wasn't
all that happy about it either.

I didn't have a lamp in my bedroom because I would just
break it. My mother's body blocked the light that came in from
the hallway. She had a hard time getting started on the Romans,
but once she got going she knew a lot about them. She sat on the
edge of my bed and held one hand with the other so her fingers
wouldn't pick at the seams in her jeans, or at loose threads in the
quilt. She smelled like something so particular I thought there
must be a name for it and I just didn't know the word yet. Her stories went on forever. I kept trying to listen and fall asleep at the
same time. Outside, Doyle's sled dogs howled and the wind in the
power lines whined.

The Roman Empire happened a long time ago. It lasted a long
time and then it declined and then it fell. We hadn't got to the fall
part yet; we were still on the Empire. There were other empires
besides the Roman one, like the Greek Empire, and the Ottoman
Empire, and the British Empire, but we hadn't got to those yet
either. Most empires last a long time, but so far none have lasted
forever. They all decline and fall.

My mother told me that Rome started as a city.
"Like Halifax?"
"Yes."
"Was there ever a Halifax Empire?"
"No."
Soon Rome became a city-state that occupied seven hills. Then
it became a kingdom, like how England used to be a kingdom.

"Why is it called a kingdom if England has a Queen?"

"Before the Queen there was a King."

My mother wished I wouldn't ask so many questions.

My father said, "The kid asks you a question, you give her a straight answer."

"A kid is a goat," my mother told him, for the fifteen-hundredth time.

"Simple Simon says go to sleep," my father said. This was as close as he ever came to an endearment.

My name is Simone.

When my mother didn't explain things well I couldn't sleep. When was conquering good and when was it not good? Rome became an empire by dividing and conquering other city-states. Divide and conquer means, if two or three other cities are friends, Rome goes and takes over the one in the middle and turns it against the others. It means, either you are Roman or you are a Barbarian. Apparently Rome still exists, but it's back to being just a city.

"Does Rome wish it was still an Empire?" I wanted to know.

My father told my mother she was explaining the Romans all wrong. He said these days it was the Americans who were building an empire. Whom are the Americans dividing? Whom are they conquering? How come the Romans could have slaves and the Americans couldn't? Who are the Barbarians now?

My mother didn't like this line of questioning.

My father said, "You can't sugar-coat Imperialism."

My mother said, "She's only six."

At school, at lunchtime, we propped up our lunchbox tops and stared at the pictures on them, pretending we were watching TV. This game made sense if you had a shiny superhero decal on your plastic lunchbox, like every other kid in the known universe. My lunchbox was painted black metal. This made me a Barbarian. After we ate, we ran around the playground with our jackets flapping behind us like capes, copying a TV show I'd never seen. There were good guys and there were bad guys in this game, but I never knew which side I was on. Isaac said it didn't matter. "You can be the robot," he said. "Just stick your arms out when you run." No one bothered to tell me that on this TV show the robot was a dog.

My father had no respect for dogs. "Pack animals," he called them. Cats were better because they were solitary, like in Aesop's fable, *The Cat Who Walked Alone*. "What's wrong with being a pack animal?" I wanted to know. The Vaughn kids were pack animals; there were so many of them you had to go along with whatever they did. "A mob mentality," was what my father accused them of having. My mother explained how the Roman Emperors built the Colosseum to control the mob. The Colosseum was like a sports stadium. Romans went there for free bread and circuses. The oldest Vaughn girl, Jeanie, said that the Romans threw Christians to the lions in the Colosseum. Lions being cats I figured this was okay. Jeanie offered to lend me a book of Bible stories. But it had pictures, so I said no. Because picture books are for babies.

Even in the daytime, my mother didn't answer questions well. "Which do you prefer?" she was always asking me, holding up two different sweaters, two different kinds of cookies, two juice glasses, the same, but with different patterns on them. I usually knew which I preferred. But rarely did I guess the right answer.

What neither of my parents seemed to have figured out was that I could read perfectly well on my own. I took books out with me when Red and I went on our walks. I never asked if I was allowed to do this. That way no one could say no. I'd already finished *The Hobbit* and was nearing the end of *Watership Down*. I planned to ask for a lamp for my birthday, so I could read myself to sleep. When I turned ten I'd get my own card at the library in town. Not that it would do me much good. My father was too busy to drop everything for a trip into town, and my mother didn't like driving.

"What's the point, anyway?" she said. "The town's so small, blink and you'll miss it."

"Blink and you won't miss it at all," my father said.

There was just no talking to these people.

When I turned twelve, I'd go to the junior high in town, which had its own library. When I turned fifteen-and-a-half I'd get my learner's permit, so when I turned sixteen, I could get my licence. Until I was free to come and go as I pleased I made do with whatever reading material we had in the house. I read through my parents' books in no particular order, so long as the shape of the book lent itself to the day's activity. The massive volumes of Will Durant's *History of Civilization* lay flat when opened; they could be read at the kitchen table while ending beans or husking corn. Virgil was pocket-sized, easily smuggled out to the ruined foundation in the northwest pasture. In summer the air was cool down there, the walls thick with vegetation. No one thought to look for me in that overgrown place. Only Red knew my clandestine destination as we passed among the cattle, *The Aeneid* in hand.

Winter nights I read covertly, flashlight under the quilts, Feather of the Fairies curled in the nook at the back of my knees. Whichever book I took to bed, I imagined I could hear the north wind whistling in through the crack that I had made with my selection — a breach in the wall of books, a book-shaped chink in the insulation.

My father's mother sent me a book and a cheque for my twelfth birthday. "But why?" I wanted to know.

"Guilt," my father said.

"Don't be ungrateful," my mother said, whether to me or to my father, I couldn't be sure.

"But she doesn't even know me," I said. As far as I could remember, my grandmother had never sent me a birthday card, let alone a present, before. She lived in Maryland or Massachusetts or Michigan maybe. Wherever it was, she wasn't really from there. She lived with a man my father called The Slime, who wasn't my father's father. As the nickname would suggest, my father detested him. The day we went down there to visit them would be the day that hell froze over. Direct quote.

"Why doesn't she come visit us?"

"Careful what you wish for," my mother warned.

For these and other reasons, the concept of grandmother completely eluded me. The concept of mother wasn't even all that clear. Other mothers told their kids what to do. My mother waited for other people to make decisions for her, which was convenient because my father's mind was always already made up. The idea that my father had a mother was laughable. As if anyone had ever told him to go to bed, as if he had ever heard the word no!

Isaac got a ten-speed for his twelfth birthday, and a pair of sneakers. Just in the nick of time, too. I'd grown an inch since the last day of grade six. Not him. He was as runty as ever. No way we'd be able to swap shoes again. In the fall we'd be bused into town for school. I was looking forward to the library. Isaac, to Shop. His ten-speed was pretty cool, but I didn't want one. He lived on a paved road; I lived on a dirt road. And besides, I had a horse.

The cheque was for two hundred dollars. The note said: *For you to start a bank account.* What do you do with a bank account? Nothing. It's to help you save money. Save it from what? *"For* what," my father corrected me. "For later, for when you grow up." I hadn't realized that growing up was going to cost me anything.

The book was *The Phantom Tollbooth* by Norton Juster. The main character was a boy named Milo, who didn't know what to do with himself — not just sometimes, but always. *Wherever he was he wished he were somewhere else, and when he got there he wondered why he'd bothered.* One day, Milo came home from school and found an enormous package in his room, containing one genuine turnpike tollbooth, some road signs and a map. Milo set up the tollbooth, drove through it and proceeded to have many clever and pun-filled adventures. He befriended a watchdog named Tock (tick-tock, tick-tock). Together they travelled through Dictionopolis to Digitopolis and eventually managed to rescue the princesses Rhyme and Reason from the Mountains of Ignorance. The best part was, no one told him it was impossible to do this until after he'd done it!

I started a bank account and read *The Phantom Tollbooth* over and over again, convinced my grandmother was sending me a secret message. This book had been written specifically for me. I always wished I were somewhere else. At school, I wished I was at home, and at home I wished I was outside. Outside, I could never decide what to do. All school year I waited for summer. After a week at home with my parents, I was exhausted from trying to figure out if I should be making myself useful or making myself scarce, and couldn't wait for school to start up again.

I wanted Isaac to read *The Phantom Tollbooth*, but I didn't want to lend the book to him, and it wasn't in the town library, and it wasn't in the school library, and when I read out sections to him he didn't get any of the jokes. He wanted me to love Metallica, but wouldn't lend me any of his albums, so basically, we were at an impasse.

"You can't live where we live and not love heavy metal," he said.

"Guess I'll have to move then," I said.

"Where will you go?"

Figures. He started taking me seriously the second I decided to leave.

One of the three road signs that came in the box with the Phantom Tollbooth advised: *HAVE YOUR DESTINATION IN MIND*. Good advice. Only, no one I knew had ever been anywhere. Except Isaac's dad and his dog Cinder, but that didn't count, because once they got wherever they were going, they turned right around and came back. And my parents, who didn't count either, because although they used to be somewhere else, the only trip they had ever taken was to here, and once they got here they just stayed. In the book, Milo decided on his destination by closing his eyes and poking his finger at the map. I decided on mine by reading every single book in the school library. This was not hard to do. Selection was limited. The town library was not much bigger than the one at school, but the Bookmobile came once a month and they were willing to take special requests.

I liked John Steinbeck's *Travels With Charlie*, but didn't want to live out of the back of a truck. Charlie sounded like a great dog, but I couldn't quite picture myself with a Standard Poodle. I liked Ernest Hemingway's safari stories, but everyone in them sounded like kind of a jerk. Africa was way too far away to plot an escape route to, and I was pretty sure I wanted to live in a city. Where we lived, when people said, "The city," they meant Halifax. I'd never been to Halifax. It was two-and-a-half hours away by car and that seemed way too close to home. The Vaughns had cousins outside of Toronto. I didn't want to move hundreds of miles away only to wind up living next to more Vaughns. The Montreal authors were my favourites. From the sounds of things they were all immigrants, or children of immigrants. Jews and Bolsheviks, whatever they were. Outsiders, I gathered. Bookish, impoverished and opinionated. I figured I'd fit right in.

"My dad goes to Montreal all the time," Isaac bragged. I asked him to ask his dad to get me a map of the city. He did, but it was a cartoon one — more of a poster than a map. Caricatures of famous Montrealers romped Godzilla-tall through the streets. Mordecai Richler was the only one I'd ever heard of, though his map-ugly mug looked nothing like it did on the back cover of *St. Urbain's Horseman*. With the cartoon map thumb-tacked above my bed, I read every Montreal author I could get my hands on, which is to say, every English Montreal author, which is to say, not very many.

For all that I had looked forward to high school, once I got there I was disappointed. The curriculum left a lot to be desired. We had the same English teacher for grades eleven and twelve, a red-nosed alcoholic who drank his lunch at the Legion Hall across the road and dictated our afternoon class notes to us with a painfully slow slur. He was afraid of the other side of his desk. We were lucky to get through one Shakespeare play a year. I got no extra credit whatsoever for memorizing A. M. Klein poems. I fell in love with, and secretly wanted to be, the nude girl in Leonard Cohen's poem, "Snow Is Falling." *She is eighteen.* Eighteen was only a matter of time. *She has straight hair.* Perfect. I started growing my straight hair long so when the time came I could hold it back to light cigarettes on the gas range. I would have to get a gas range. I would have to take up smoking and procure a wine-coloured carpet. No problem. *She speaks no Montreal language.* What was a Montreal language? I was dying to know.

A big part of my Escape To Montreal plan revolved around getting into university. My parents were all for higher education. Too bad they hadn't planned ahead for mine. Our farm wasn't exactly turning a profit. My grades weren't great, due to my reading all the wrong things, so scholarships were out of the question. I went to the guidance counsellor for advice. He gave me an aptitude test. "Mechanical Engineering," the results suggested. "I was thinking Classics, or Art History," I said. "Suit yourself," he sighed, and handed over the student loan applications.

I set about supplementing my birthday present bank account with money from odd jobs. Jeanie Vaughn had already cornered the babysitting market. My father hired Jack and Isaac to help out on our haying crew, but wouldn't pay me to do the same work. Family farms are the last bastions of child labour. I went down to the Doyle place and picked up a swing shift driving forklift at the sawmill. When Isaac found out what Doyle was paying me, he quit my father's haying crew and came down to work at the sawmill too. My father was so mad he stopped speaking to me. I didn't notice at first. The difference between him speaking to me and not speaking to me was that negligible.

By the time I was seventeen, I was convinced that I'd fallen hopelessly far behind in life. That's yet another detrimental side effect of reading the classics at a young age. It seemed as though people in classical times acheived so much more than we did now and died younger. Alexander the Great was king of the world by twenty. I ought to have marched on Gaul, at least.

My accomplishments were more modest. I'd convinced Red to trot, canter, and then gallop — even though I barely weighed 110 pounds. I'd learned to drive a truck, a tractor, a forklift, and a snowmobile. I'd managed the grades necessary to get into univer- .

sity in Montreal. By the time the acceptance letter came I'd saved up almost enough money to pay for the first year's tuition, secured student loans for the rest, grown my hair to shoulder length, and taken up smoking.

I'd tried to get Isaac to apply to university too, but he'd said no way. Every week he had a different plan: the forestry service, the coast guard, or ship mechanic, maybe, or long-haul trucking like his dad.

"You could study those things in university," I said.

"You can be the robot," he said. "Just remember to stick out your arms."

Whatever he thought about my leaving, he was pretty great about talking his dad into helping me do it. The Monday after high school graduation, I stood out at the end of our driveway with two suitcases, two boxes of books, and a typewriter. The books were the only thing my parents were choked to see go. Arguing over them saved us from discussing many other things.

In my backwoods Cinderella escape fantasy, Isaac's dad would pull up in his big rig and whisk me away. In reality, it was Isaac who came to get me. He had to keep his pick-up truck running or else it would stall. "Dad's loading down at the Spa Springs," he said. "We'll meet him there." I was relieved to hear we'd be hauling mineral water to Montreal. If it had been lobster, everything I owned would have smelled like seafood for the rest of my life.

"Where're your folks?" Isaac asked, when we were ready to roll.

"We said good-bye after breakfast," I lied. After breakfast I'd gone out to the barn, leaned my head on Red's brown barrel chest and listened to him breathe.

Isaac and I hugged good-bye on the loading dock of the Spa Springs Mineral Water bottling plant, his pick-up idling in the loading zone, his dad waiting in the rig's air-conditioned cab. We'd known each other all our lives, but as far as I could recall, Isaac and I had never hugged before. His chin came up to about my collarbone. His dad was a big man. I suspected that the minute I left home, Isaac would outgrow me.

"Are we going to keep in touch?" I asked him.

"I doubt it," he said, and handed me a mixed Metallica tape. "There's some Mötley Crü on there too," he grinned. Great.

"Not in my cab," his dad said as soon as he saw it. We listened to Gordon Lightfoot instead, and Neil Young, and Johnny Cash. Maybe he *had* been in a band. I didn't know how to ask.

The drive took fourteen hours, and a pack of cigarettes each. After less than an hour on the road, every single thing I saw was new to me. Cinder the dog was long gone, but I thought about him a lot. Every new thing I saw, I realized, he'd beaten me to it: that sign, that diner, that cliff, that terrifying S-curve, that wide-mouthed river.

Montreal was more beautiful than the cartoon map made it out to be. And bigger. And all the neighbourhoods were further apart than I'd thought they'd be when Isaac's dad and I had sat poring over an AAA map in a topless diner at a truck stop just shy of Saint-Jean-Port-Jolie. He'd circled the university, which startled me. Until that moment it hadn't occurred to me to wonder where it was. He wrote out the address of a warehouse were I could store my stuff until I found a place to live, and he suggested some good neighbourhoods where I could hunt for an apartment.

"How will I know if the apartments are for rent or not?" I asked, with the sinking feeling that for the next few months I'd be reduced to asking many more, equally stupid questions. He told me that if an apartment were for rent it would have a sign in the window that said: *À Louer*. This system seemed improbably simple.

I didn't believe that was the way they'd do things in the city. But Isaac's dad was right. The *À Louer* signs were everywhere. Just like in Nova Scotia, where you see signs at the end of every other driveway: *Blueberries, Corn, Pies, Worms, Car for Sale, Free Gravel*.

The university didn't look anything like what a lifetime of reading novels had led me to expect. There was no campus, no grass, no quad, no paths through green. Most of the buildings appeared to have been built for other purposes. The Arts and Sciences building closely resembled a penitentiary, and the Fine Arts building, a parking garage. The Art History classrooms were hot, and uncommonly dry. There was a musty smell, even on the first day of school. In the cramped narrow rows of shabby auditorium seats, there was no room for extra books or bags or restless legs. The seats surrendered to you when you sat, but folded up behind you quickly when you stood to leave, as if they couldn't wait to get rid of you. At the front of the classroom a forlorn lectern waited, poised at the edge of an expanse of hard, white wall.

The lights dimmed. Two slides were thrust ahead; light from two projectors sliced though the nervous, first-day atmosphere. A million specks of dust were exposed. The slides advanced. Warm colours, dry earth and intoxicating tones — the weathered stone of ancient Rome hung suspended in mid-air. Professor Azar ventured out from behind the lectern to point to some detail, to draw our attention to some historic trick of light playing itself out on the classroom wall. Her fingers traced the contours of volutes, led us through mythic narratives carved in bas-relief. With the glare of the projectors in her eyes, her brow would furrow. Squinting, she'd smile at us. Dazzling. Histories stacked in stone melted and bent across her body. Tons of travertine toyed with the hues of her complexion. Finely-drawn architectural models became abstracted in the patterns of her dress. Entire frescos, only recently rescued from the obscurity of centuries, were lost again in the dense blackness of her hair.

My first semester in Montreal whizzed by in a blur of ancient history mixed with new names, faces and facts. I'd passed high school French with *pas de problème*, but couldn't understand a word of the Montreal languages now swirling around me. Even the English was strange to me. I kept my mouth shut and did my best not to let on that I was a total hick. Where I'd come from, roads were named after the people who lived on them. In this city, every other street was named after a saint. I'd had no idea there were so many saints. Or so many different ways to say things. I'd never written a proper essay before, according to Professor Azar. Each sentence had a structure, each paragraph had a purpose, and each argument was won or lost according to laws of rhetoric as yet unknown to me. I'd never had my own apartment before, with a key and lease and my name in the phonebook. I'd never owned my own dishes, or done laundry at a *buanderie*, or taken public transportation. The Metro was a marvel. I stood swaying amid thousands of conversations hurtling through dark tunnels on black rubber wheels.

Soon, everyone around me was talking about going home for Christmas. On the Metro, on the Parc bus, in the halls at school, at the bi-weekly openings at the art gallery in the Fine Arts building. Some people spoke of the upcoming holidays grudgingly, but many seemed quite happy about the prospect of spending time with family. I couldn't imagine it. I couldn't remember the last time we'd celebrated anything at our house. "Waste of a good tree," according to my father. "Capitalist invention," according to my mother. The older my parents got, the more alike they sounded. The more they repeated themselves the easier they were to converse with, in some ways. A phone call every few months produced no new questions, just the same old sentences. Fine by me.

My first winter in Montreal, the daytime temperature didn't rise above minus fifteen degrees Celsius for five whole weeks. This seemed insane by Nova Scotia standards, but people kept telling me that it was normal. Nights it went down to minus twenty-five or less. Heat, or the lack thereof, was all I could think of. What had passed as a winter jacket in Nova Scotia was barely sufficient to withstand the Montreal cold, and did nothing whatsoever against the wind. New clothes were not in my budget. Staying in didn't help. Someone from a warm place must have built my building. I cursed that ill-informed immigrant to Montreal — from Portugal, or Greece maybe — for laying down tile floors in the hallway, bathroom and kitchen. The avocado-coloured refrigerator kept food slightly warmer than the rest of the apartment. It rumbled to life at odd hours of the night, loud and empty as a cargo plane. I heard it all in that place. Sneezes, grunts and telephone conversations. Country music, salsa and bad hip-hop. The guy upstairs cross-dressed; night after night he practiced his unsteady stiletto gait, traipsing heavily over my head. The girl next door turned tricks, for cash or beer or kicks I couldn't say. Five in the morning, five in the afternoon, fifteen minutes max, a different guy each time, her headboard bucking into the wall behind mine. The walls were too thin for insulation and none of the windows closed properly. Snow drifted under the back door until I stuffed in a bath towel. I could only afford to heat one room. I chose the bedroom because the door closed. Ensconced in a cocoon of blankets, bath towels, coats and sweaters, I read incessantly. Books on Pompeii and Herculaneum mostly. Suffocation by fiery heat and hot cinder, while outside snow fell in slow motion. The seconds rained down like giant pieces of ash. I couldn't wait for school to start up again.

Work, work, work — that's all farm people ever do. Even in the city. It was far harder to find work in the metropolis of Montreal than it had been in middle-of-nowhere rural Nova Scotia. French, or lack thereof, was the least of my problems. I'd never had to ask for work from someone I didn't know before. None of my forklift-driving, hay-bale tossing, hen-beheading, green-bean-ending, horseback-riding, cattle-round-up skills seemed applicable to what few job options were available to an eighteen-year-old anglophone Art History major. I tried to wait-ress all of once; I didn't last the day.

Eventually I stumbled into a part-time job in the university library. Literally, stumbled. I thought I was standing in the line to apply for in-course bursaries but wound up scoring the most cov-eted manual labour job available in the university: shelving books. I spent all my spare time in the library anyway. Now I got paid to lift books, shift them, cart them around, find them, fix them and keep them in order. My fingers cracking from the dry pages, I maxed out my library card on non-required reading.

It took me months to notice that giving the appearance of working hard was decidedly un-cool, at least that's the impression I got in the Fine Arts building, where most of my Art History classes were held. I attempted to mask my self-imposed study regime, made efforts to socialize, to slack off, to not raise my hand in class, to not take notes, to hang out at art openings after school, to skip some classes altogether for matinée screenings of obscure films with subtitles at the Cinéma du Paris. The ironic thing to do after a film or an afternoon at the museum, I soon learned, was to go for 99-cent plates of spaghetti and pitchers of cheap beer at the

Peel Pub. I could pretend at these rebellions. Just not for long.

If I hadn't arrived in Montreal in the middle of summer, by the end of my first winter I would not have believed summer possible. The very idea of spring sounded like a vicious rumour at first — too good to be true. The melt progressed at the painstakingly slow pace of an archaeological excavation. A whole winter's worth of dog shit was revealed, one turd at a time. Beneath that, last fall's leaves. The buds were waiting on the trees, right where we'd left them; bare legs under those jeans, sundresses in closets waiting to bloom. On the first day the temperature rose to hover just above zero, the line-up at the Parc bus stop looked like this: an old woman in a fur coat and patent-leather purse, a young woman in a jean jacket and Walkman, a middle-aged guy in shorts and a McGill sweatshirt, me in my only coat carrying a slippery stack of oversized art books.

I read up on how to write an essay and managed a second-semester A from Professor Azar for a paper vaingloriously entitled, "From Claude to Corot: Northern Influences on the Veduta Tradition in the Roman Campagna." The Roman Campagna became more real to me than the city around me. From reading and writing late into the night, layers of past landscapes had become as confused in my head as the contents of a slide carousel spilled onto a classroom floor. The Cloaca Maxima drained the ground water of ancient Rome into the stream that powered the sawmill down behind the Doyle place. Lonely aqueducts and broken villas situated themselves in the pastures of my parents' farm.

One sodden, grey, spring evening I saw Professor Azar on the Parc bus. In the rush-hour crowd she was no Pompeian wall painting, no profile fit for an Etruscan urn. Youngish, smallish, jostled, weighed down by a rain-stained coat. Someone called out to her, "Vita!" They kissed, both cheeks. I was not prepared to see her like this, kissing, and real. I retreated into the anonymous throng at the back of the bus.

When people in Montreal found out that I grew up in rural Nova Scotia, they said things like: "Oh, it's so beautiful there." I shrugged. "Nice place to visit, but I wouldn't want to live there." While everyone else in Montreal seemed to be conspiring to get out of the city for the summer, I was busy looking for ways to stay. The only way I could keep my job at the university library was to enrol in summer classes. The choices were limited. I wound up with Seventeenth-Century Poetry and Prose. I was thrilled to discover that the seventeenth-century was a neoclassical period. I'd never read Johnson or Bacon or Milton or Donne, but I had read the same classics as them. This put me slightly ahead of the few English Lit majors in the class, which put me in their bad books, I gathered, from the looks they shot my way each and every time I raised my hand. I couldn't help it. It seemed that every text we studied had borrowed something from Ovid's *Metamorphoses*, Virgil's *Eclogues*, or Horace's *Epodes*. *Beatus ille qui procul negotiis — Happy the man who, far away from business cares, like the pristine race of mortals, works his ancestral acres with his steers....* No wonder everyone I met in the city thought farm life was romantic — this myth had persisted for centuries. The Pastoral, they call it. I was fairly certain that I was the only person in my class who had ever ventured into a pasture to milk a cow.

My faux-Mediterranean tiled apartment was almost as hot in the summer as it had been cold in winter. I climbed the Mountain often — a book in hand — in search of a cool place amid the vegetation. Mounted police patrolled the park. Big men all, but their horses plodded board-stiff slow except when spurred to round up owners of dogs running off-leash.

From a distance the Mountain disguised itself as any one of the seven ancient hills of Rome. From certain vantage points I could easily confuse Montreal with Professor Azar's Rome, a phantom image projected over the real city below. Evenings I searched through the stacks of books that lined the baseboards of my apartment, sometimes searching for titles that weren't there, missing my parents' wall of shelves. Nights I barely slept, my apartment airless, my head full of reading, shapes and scenes shifting in the whirring, clicking jumble of my mind.

I was so relieved when school finally started up again in the fall that I bought myself a scuffed leather briefcase at a thrift shop to celebrate. It came pre-ink-stained. One of my co-workers at the library asked me if it came with a matching tweed jacket. "No, do you have one I could borrow?" By the end of September, I had noted at least four other students in the Fine Arts building sporting similarly worn leather briefcases. I was thrilled. For the first time in my life, I'd successfully anticipated a fashion trend.

There was a guy in my second-year History of Hellenistic Sculpture class who actually wore an ascot. He was the same age as me, if not younger, with such long fingers that for most of the semester I assumed he was a piano player. But no, it turned out he was a costume designer. We fell into conversation in the smoking section outside the Fine Arts building the week between the end of classes and the beginning of exams.

"Adrian," he said, proffering a long hand sporting a signet ring on the pinkie finger. "Like the Emperor," he said. He looked nothing like Hadrian. Rather more like the young Antinous, Hadrian's favourite, Hadrian's folly.

"Simone," I said.

"Like Nina?" he asked.

"Oh, I don't know..." I said vaguely, unwilling to admit that I had no idea who he was talking about. I'd never heard of a Simone Nina. In grade school the kids had called me Simon, Simple Simon, Simon Says. Since university I'd been aiming for a Simone more like Weil, or de Beauvoir.

"Well, from the neck up you look like a John Singer Sergeant," he said. Note to self: Look up John Singer Sergeant. Adrian claimed he was studying classical statuary to learn about drapery, though clearly he was in it for the nudes. He was an imperious little prick, but I'd been in Montreal for over a year already, too long without a friend.

All of Adrian's plans were lopsided somehow. He'd design the costumes for an entire opera down to the last detail and then say, "Okay, all we need is a libretto. Could you take care of that?" He'd plan fantastic dinner parties, replete with themes dress-codes and hand-printed menus, and then call his hapless guests personally to say they'd have to chip in fifty bucks each. I went along with most of these plans anyway. My apartment was getting unbearably cold again and most of Adrian's theatrics gave me a destination. Setting, as he said, is key.

One night he invited me over to his cousin Colin's place for a few beers. In Adrian-world, "a few beers" could mean anything. Once, not long after we first met, we went for a pitcher at a bar on the Main and wound up — late, late at night — shooting a super-8 film at some guy's scary loft in an utterly deserted corner of Old Montreal that I've never since been able to locate.

"What's the occasion?" I asked.

"No occasion, I just want you to meet him."

"Why?"

"He's a real character." This from a boy who wore ascots and signet rings.

"Colin's the black sheep in the family," was all Adrian would say.

In a family of theatre folk, painters, playwrights and musicians, Colin was a bricklayer. All you had to do was shake his hand to know it. His forearms bulged Popeye-style. Both his elbows sported spider-web tattoos.

"Hey, that's some firm handshake," Colin said to me.

"Crush or be crushed," I said.

"Sorry about that."

"Simone's a farm girl, she can take it," Adrian pronounced. Colin asked where I was from and when I told him Nova Scotia he said, "Oh, it's so beautiful there," just like everyone else did, but he looked like he'd fit right in there. He wore a plaid shirt and grey work pants, and drank Keith's and strung his curses together in basically the same order as every guy I'd gone to high school with.

"Isn't he great?" Adrian nudged me every time Colin left the room to get another beer. I remained non-committal. At some drunken point in the evening it occurred to me that maybe Adrian thought of me as a girl version of Colin. In which case we had a problem. Perhaps the stink of my plaid-shirted past still clung to me. Or, worse yet, perhaps Adrian thought I was an effete boy version of Colin, and was secretly into me. I'd had just about enough of Adrian's blue-collar slumming and was struggling vainly to extricate myself from the depths of a fit-for-the-alleyway couch, when Colin came back into the room with yet more beer and said, apropos of nothing in particular as far as I could tell, "Anyone know how to work a woodstove? Cause my bike mechanic's apartment's up for rent. It's a funky little place, and the rent's really low, only thing is, it's wood heat and no one seems to know how to work a woodstove anymore. Anyone interested?"

I raised my hand.

Adrian's cousin Colin's bike mechanic's apartment was on the ground floor of a dilapidated place on the corner of a back alley and a narrow brick-paved street I'd never noticed before. The street was closed to cars. The bike mechanic claimed it had been turned into a pedestrians only zone on the occasion of the Pope's visit to Montreal, but the woman who lived upstairs said they closed it to cars after a truck driver crushed a girl against the side of a building. I wondered which building. Was it our building? I didn't dare ask. If the place was haunted I didn't want to know. The ceilings were low. The broad-board hardwood floors rolled and pitched, the bulbous plaster walls cracked and sagged, the copper pipes bent at odd angles around doorways and shuddered down the dark hall. The bathtub was almost too long for me to touch my toes to the faucet end. This apartment was warmer than my previous place, but only just barely. And only if you sat right next to the woodstove. Yes, there really was a woodstove. In the middle of Montreal. At the end of twentieth century. It was rustic all right. I wondered if my parents would love it or hate it. Hate it probably. The woodstove in question wasn't a very efficient one. Five cord a winter it took to heat that place, but the shed only had room for two, which meant three loads per winter. You can take a girl out of the country. But she'll still wind up piling firewood.

One of the weirdest things about living in a city, if you don't grow up in one, is how many people there are. All day, every day, wall-to-wall people coming and going, just walking around out there. There were no cars on my narrow street, but lots of pedestrians. I set up shop on the front stoop, doing most of my schoolwork there, smoking cigarettes and reading from my endless supply of library books. I was the opposite of a *flâneur*. I sat in one place and watched the city walk by.

Every evening around 6 PM, a blonde girl walked by my place wearing a floral skirt, every evening a different one. This girl had dozens of floral skirts. And a dog. Every time the blonde girl and her dog walked by, the dog peed on the corner of my building. "Mingus!" she admonished him, but he was a dog of habit. If I happened to be sitting outside while Mingus was pissing on my building the girl would look horrified and apologize. After a while I started to take it as a compliment, how insistent he was on claiming my corner as his territory. Finally, I said, "Oh, it's all right, better him than the drunk guys who piss on my building."

Her name was Julie. I came to think of her as my imaginary friend. She was real, and we were becoming real friends, but it was nothing like how I'd imagined being friends with a girl would be. We were opposites in every way. She was Franco-Ontarian, with perfect French and perfect English and perfect teeth and long, wavy, blonde hair. She had a gym membership, a flair for fashion and home decoration, and a way with people. I was none of the above. I didn't own a single skirt, let alone a floral one. After graduation, Julie had travelled around South-East Asia. She had lived in Malaysia for four months. "Floral skirts are a dime a dozen there," she said. Practically everything in her apartment was teak. Except her dog Mingus, of course. He was part birch, part mahogany.

Julie had a real job. She worked for a software company down in Griffintown. I was entering my final year of university. Julie and I often wound up on the Parc bus from Mile End to downtown together. She wore floral skirts even in winter. My schedule was more flexible than hers, so sometimes I took Mingus out for walks at odd hours of the day. Sometimes I took him back to my place to keep me company while I ploughed through coursework and required readings. I had stupidly put off all my twentieth-century

Art History requirements until my last year. Professor Azar had strongly suggested I take some cultural theory classes as well. I'd signed up for Feminist Practices in Poststructuralist Theory and soon regretted it. The feminist part seemed like a good idea, but the *post* part of poststructuralist confused the hell out of me. Technology in Contemporary Art was no better. Even if the professor hadn't had an impenetrable Austrian accent and a speech impediment that made him repeat every single *b* and *p* a half dozen times, I wouldn't have known what he was talking about. Video art? I had yet to own a television. Cyberspace? I was still typing my term papers on the same typewriter that I'd transported to Montreal in the back of Isaac's dad's tractor-trailer load of Spa Springs mineral water.

"What the hell is a p-p-p-p-p-pixel?" I asked Mingus. He answered these sorts of rhetorical questions with cryptic raises of eyebrows or ears. While I struggled to make sense of Marshall McLuhan and Donna Haraway he lay at my feet on the floor, watching the door, waiting for Julie. I swear he could hear her coming from the moment she got off the bus, four blocks away. His ears would go up and his tail would start thumping the hardwood as footsteps headed his way. This was happy. This was the most home I'd ever known.

E arly in December, Julie invited me to a cocktail party at her place. I showed up unfashionably early, wearing a pair of cowboy boots I'd bought recently at a thrift shop, in a vain attempt to appear ironic, and a pair of jeans I'd owned since high school. Julie was wearing a floral skirt as per usual, and a sleeveless top so simply cut I suspected that it was expensive. We both pretended I'd come early to help her set up. I busied myself in the kitchen, arranging cheeses on a platter. Julie came in holding a selection of slinky tops on wooden hangers.

"I was thinking," she said. "Either of these two would go great with your retro-look jeans." Honestly. Julie's so good. In some other life she'd be tending to lepers. It wouldn't surprise me if she adopted half-a-dozen orphans tomorrow.

Eventually other guests arrived. On time, in Montreal, is almost an hour late. Every single person I spoke to that evening seemed smart, friendly, attractive and successful. Perhaps this was because they were all drinking Cosmopolitans, an innately sophisticated beverage. Or maybe it was just because, like Julie, they were older than me, out of school a few years already and, from the looks of their purposeful hairdos and brand-new blue jeans, quite gainfully employed. I was both impressed and discouraged by the high calibre of these friends of Julie's. On the one hand, I was in good company. On the other hand, how long could our friendship — predicated as it was on the insistence with which her dog peed in the same place every day — possibly last?

Most of the people at the party already knew each other. At least half of them seemed more inclined to speak French than English. My French was improving, but my comprehension had yet to reach fast-paced cocktail banter rate. Names for people and things slipped in and out of my head too fast for me to carry on a conversation. I wound up sitting on the floor in the diningroom with my back against an ornate, antique, Malaysian armoire that probably cost more than my first year of university. I ashed cigarette after cigarette as discreetly as possible into a gigantic potted plant that surely outweighed me. Mingus came over and sat down next to me and the two of us watched — like kids at the top of the stairs — as the grown-ups went about having their party.

After a while, a guy showed up who looked as out of place as

I did. "Who's that, Mingus?" I asked. He raised one eyebrow, then the other, the dog equivalent of a shrug. The new arrival had long, wavy hair right out of the seventies. His glasses looked like something you'd be forced to wear in Shop for safety purposes. He did the double-kiss-on-the-cheek thing with Julie in the hallway. He waded through the fashionable crowd without stopping to talk. Maybe he doesn't know anyone here either, I thought. At the bar he poured a glass of red wine instead of mixing a Cosmo. Interesting. Minugs's tail started to thump on the floorboards as the out-of-place guy headed right for our hideout by the Malaysian armoire.

"*Salut, Mingus*," he said and sat down on the floor with us.

"*En veux-tu un?*" I offered him a cigarette.

"Thanks," he said in English — apparently unimpressed by my spectacular use of vernacular. He said his name was Theo. In French, with loud music playing, Theo sounded like Day-O. As in: *Daylight come and me wan' go home*. In order to remember his name, which I really wanted to do, I had to keep that damn Day-O song in my head. Calypso music generally makes me crave rum. I would have gotten quite drunk had I not been so reluctant to leave the safe haven of Mingus, the Malaysian armoire, and the potted-tree ashtray. Theo didn't know anyone else at the party either. Except Mingus, who hung out with us all night. Without dogs or smoking sections, how would we ever meet anyone?

I had a screaming hangover the next day, and a term paper due, and exams to study for — if I lived that long. The paper was going to be about the invention of the classical by early Renaissance antiquarians, if only I could get my brain to function. I'd been out late and slept late and after all that time without a fire going it was freezing in my apartment. Heating with wood, you literally have to keep the home fires burning. I'd only just started to warm the place up when the phone rang, early in the afternoon. For a second, I had no idea where the horrible ringing sound was coming from. It occurred to me that it might be coming from inside my head. And then, very briefly, I thought the sound might split my head open and kill me dead.

"Who is this?" I mumbled, my tongue thick as a welcome mat.

"Theo," the phone said. Day-O.

Theo invited me to breakfast at a diner I'd never been to, on Laurier East.

"Wow, this place is a real greasy spoon," I said. Theo had never heard that expression before. His English was like Julie's: perfect except when it came to expressions. The more I tried to explain what a "greasy spoon" was, the funnier it sounded. Finally our eggs arrived and Theo said, "It's greasy more than just spoon."

We walked back to my place after our afternoon breakfast, heads down, eyes squinting against a cold much colder than the cold we'd set out in. Wind tunnelled between the boxy, grey, textile factory buildings on de Gaspé and Casgrain. A few flakes of snow landed on my eyelashes. I looked up and didn't recognize a thing. As if we'd fallen into a foreign city for a moment. And then we rounded onto Fairmount Street, and there was a familiar block of Saint-Laurent.

It was cold enough in my apartment for our breath to hang white in the air like empty speech balloons. "You might as well keep your coat on," I said, opening the stove door, opening the damper, laying some more kindling on the morning's coals and slamming out the back door for more wood from the shed. To his credit Theo did not say: Wow, you heat with a woodstove! Or any of the other predictably incredulous things first-time visitors have been known to intone. He didn't offer to help either. Smart. I would have thrown him out on his ear.

"Heats up fast," was all he said, once I had the fire going.

"It gets really cold at night though," I said.

"No," Theo said. "I don't think it will."

Adrian couldn't stand Theo. Either that or he wanted him for himself. "He's too butch for you," he said.

"No, he's too butch for *you*," I said. "*I'm* too butch for you. Jesus, this dishtowel is too butch for you. This dishtowel could beat you to a pulp."

"Alright, alright." Adrian fluttered his crazy-long fingers like a silent film starlet.

Theo didn't care much for Adrian either, not that he ever said a word against him. Or against anyone else, for that matter. Theo was the calmest person I'd ever met. For the first few months, this unnerved me. It illustrated to me just how tightly wound I was. He was almost a decade older than me, but that didn't explain the gap in our temperaments. I doubted time would make me any more placid. If I ever became even half as patient as Theo it would be a drastic improvement.

I was hurtling through university at a breakneck pace. Literally. Five classes and twenty-five hours a week working at the library — my neck was a mess. My whole left side really.

"What's your hurry?" Theo asked, kneading the perma-lump lodged deep in behind my left shoulder blade. He had studied Art History too, but in French at UQAM, and his focus had been on more recent history — Art Nouveau, The Arts and Crafts Movement, Bauhaus. He fell in love with design. And then he started to built things. Furniture mostly. His apartment was practically empty except for his unsold creations, which included the most elegant desks and chairs and dressers I'd ever seen. He'd spend months building them and then he couldn't bear to part with them. We spent most nights at my place, because if I didn't keep the woodstove going, the pipes would freeze. Theo read with his feet directly on the stove and I worked on my class assignments propped up in bed under layers of blankets, with books and papers splayed out all around me. He read incredibly slowly, even in French. I read with a pencil, three books at once, taking notes as I went.

"I could bring over a desk for you," Theo had offered on more than one occasion.

"I get some of my best work done in bed," I said. I did try to move my mess to the floor before Theo came to bed, but sometimes we'd roll over onto a book or get stabbed by a stray pen in the night or wake up with the ink from words scrawled on lost index cards tattooed onto our backs or thighs.

"Okay, you're officially more of a bachelor than I am," Theo said one night when he found a hammer in my bed.

"Sorry, usually I store that in the couch."

Theo didn't have a couch because he hadn't found just the right one yet. My couch came from the alley. The magazine rack in his bathroom held Lee Valley Hardware catalogues. Goethe's *Maxims and Reflections* graced the back of my toilet. When we ate at my place, I cooked without looking, talking non-stop, gesticulating with a chef's knife in hand. When Theo had me over for dinner at his place I made sure to snack beforehand because it took him so long to cook; he measured every ingredient exactly and cut each slice of each vegetable precisely. His plates were bone china. The sheets on his bed were three-hundred threads per square inch. Champagne tastes minus the pretension. He worked construction to support his meticulous habits. Custom work, of course. Kitchens and bathrooms. The money rooms, he called them.

"How can you stand to spend so much time at my place?" I asked him. On top of the persistent cold, and the dirt and dust that the woodstove generated, there was no sink in the bathroom, the kitchen ceiling had recently spawned two strange water stains, and the plaster walls sported numerous lightening-forked cracks, each one longer than my arm.

"There're too many things wrong with your place to even bother fixing them. It's like a vacation from home renovation!"

He had more than enough work elsewhere. Many of the old apartments on the Plateau were being renovated. These were the places where the immigrants and Bolsheviks I'd read novels about in high school had once lived. Everywhere we walked, Theo had stories of the guts of buildings. The inside of one place on Saint-Dominique, he said, was covered in murals. A mother and daughter duo had painted every surface, even the risers of the stairs.

"It's a shame the new owners destroyed all that," I said.

"They had to," he said. "There was mould underneath the paint, and rot underneath that."

In another place on Laval Street, he'd installed floor-to-ceiling bookshelves along three walls of the front room. "Wow, a library," I said.

"You mean a *bibliothèque*."

"Not a *librairie*. A library." I told him about the wall of books at my parents' house, the rough plank shelves my father had nailed into place. He told me about the cabinetry course he planned to take in the fall. I'd never heard anyone speak with such passion about dovetailing before. I asked him about that party at Julie's place, the night we'd met. "So, were you coming over to see me or the dog or the antique armoire?"

"Julie made me come to that party," he said.

"That doesn't answer my question."

"She'd been telling me about you for months."

"She never told me about you."

"She wasn't sure," he said. "That's why she had the party, so we could meet and figure it out for ourselves."

Late that spring, as soon as the snow and the slush and the winter's worth of dog shit was gone, Theo moved into my tiny, falling-down apartment on the brick-paved street. He was over all the time anyway. It seemed silly to keep paying rent on his apartment for naught but his furniture to live there. Living together was not much different, except now we had an excessive amount of furniture and no time to rearrange it all. I was mired in my last semester of my final year, studying for final exams, agonizing over my last term papers ever, nostalgic already for my job at the library that I'd have to give up soon. Theo was busy with spring's fresh crop of outdoor work — most of it paying. Somehow he got roped into building a rock wall *pro bono* in the back garden of his mother's place up in the Laurentians.

"Are there that many rocks in her garden?"

"No, she bought the rocks."

Where I come from a rock wall springs up in the space between two fields as the result of clearing them.

Julie totally denied fixing Theo and me up until we moved in together. Then she took full credit. "But how did you even think of it?" I wanted to know. "I mean, we're so different."

"Are you kidding? You two are exactly alike."

"Name one way in which we're even remotely alike."

"Neither one of you has any idea how different you are from everyone else, for one thing."

"We're misfits, you mean."

"Individuals," she said.

Come to think of it, I'd always bonded with the oddest ball

available. Adrian, for example. And skinny, talks-too-much Isaac. All those perfectly good Vaughn kids to play with right down the road from me, and my best friend was Red the horse.

"You two make a good team," Julie said. "Take it from me, I'm stuck with Team Bozo." Julie had been transferred within her company, to work on something called the Tradeshow Team. "Tradeshow is part of Marketing, but Events is part of Sales," she explained. When she got going talking about her work sometimes I could barely understand her. The acronyms don't help. NAB, SIGGRAPH, ICA. She'd travelled a lot, but only to tedious places: Vegas, San Antonio, San Jose.

"So why do you do it?"

"The last tradeshow of the season is in Amsterdam."

"Last week Mingus walked past here with one of his dog sitters," I told her. "It felt like he was having an affair."

"He hates it. It's too much moving around for him."

"I'm around this summer, he could stay with me."

"Are you sure?"

"No, but let's try it."

I was scared to death of the responsibility, but I hated the thought of Mingus couch surfing. School was over, I had no work and Theo planned to spend the summer in Vermont, helping his older brother Earl finish building a house he'd been working on for a few years now. Theo had invited Mingus and me to come down to Vermont for the summer too, but his brother's set-up sounded a bit too back-to-the-land for my tastes.

"How do you have a brother named Earl, anyway?"

"Half-brother. It's a long story."

Theo and Earl were born eight years, two marriages, and two languages apart. Their mother, Thérèse, was Québécoise. Tiny-boned and ancient as an insect trapped in amber, her hair a shade of red not known to occur in nature, she had been a beauty in her day. She put herself through nursing school with a part time job at a glove factory and developed a knack for marrying men with great potential. Earl's father was an American, enrolled in law school at McGill when Thérèse met him. He had the potential to be a great lawyer, the way he argued, but instead he wound up needing one, and then another. "That's why Earl went back-to-the-land," Theo said. "No one there to tell him what to do."

We saw more than enough of Theo's mother. She was over at our place all the time checking up on us. I'd yet to meet Theo's father, and, I gathered, I wasn't likely to. He was Québécois, fresh out of a BSC at Université de Montréal when he met Thérèse. He'd had no plans for law school until she talked him into it. He made it through, with her considerable assistance. And then Theo came along. And then his father used his legalese to leave Thérèse, Theo and Earl for a plump young notary public at the *hôtel de ville*.

"If you tell me he went on to practice family law I will just scream."

"So I won't tell you," Theo shrugged.

Theo had never learned to drive. Wise, considering the traffic in Montreal. Usually, when he needed a lift somewhere, he enlisted his mother. On the road Thérèse was a menace to public safety. Off the road she was an expert in not paying for parking. *"J'suis vielle,"* she said, brandishing her out-of-date handicapped parking pass at the police. There was no way Theo's mother was going to drive him down to Vermont. She'd made the trip once before, when her grandson Daniel was born. The drive had been too long for her, the last leg on dirt roads too harrowing. When she had arrived she found the conditions more abhorrent than she could have imagined. Earl and Tess were living in a trailer while they built their house. Thérèse was a lady, Montreal born and bred. She wouldn't partake of the chemical toilet or spend the night on an air mattress. Earl had driven her back to Montreal in her car and returned to Vermont by bus. Thérèse had yet to forgive him for bringing her only grandchild into a world where there was nowhere for her to walk or wash or sit or rest or lay her head.

I decided to borrow Julie's car and drive Theo down to Vermont myself. I didn't want to spend all summer in the country, but a day would be all right. We'd take Mingus. It would be a family outing. We set out early. It was the first time I'd been off the island of Montreal since Isaac's dad had driven me over the Champlain Bridge in his big rig. We drove through the Champlain Lake Islands. By South Hero Island, Theo reported, Mingus was looking sick to death of the car. "As long as he's not sick to death *in* the car," I said. We were surrounded by open space — farmyards, fields, woods and hills — but there was nowhere to stop, really. In the city, every open green space is public property. It's the opposite in the country. All land is fenced or posted. *No Trespassing. No Hunting.* Finally we found a graveyard. Apologies to the dead of South Hero. We enjoyed your tended acre. Mingus especially. Off like a shot. For fifteen minutes as far as he could get from the car.

Underneath a particularly weepy willow, I found a squat white marker stone engraved with a single word: CHARLES.

"OVER HERE Mingus," I called. "SIT."

Dogs know when you're taking their picture.

CHARLES Mingus. One soulful dog.

Theo's driving instructions were vague at best. Get off the highway at Montpellier. Don't cross the bridge. Drive on the two-lane highway for half an hour. Hang a left onto an even smaller road, follow its twists and turns until the fork at the *Drink 7-Up* general store. Drive pretty much straight uphill for a few miles until you pass the creamery. Then take the first dirt road to your right, more uphill, up, up, through spruce and sugar maple. Where the dirt road veers right toward the high plains, take a left. The Baxter Road was the narrowest dirt road I'd ever seen. Even narrower than the Sloane Road. Not on the map. Not maintained by the county. No snowplough in winter. In summer it's a sun-dappled tunnel of green. When you get near enough, the dogs will start barking.

Sure enough, we came around a blind bend out of a shady hollow up into a full sun stretch and there were the dogs barking. There were Tess and Earl waiting. "So few cars up here," Tess said, hugging me like a long-lost relation.

"Heard you from three, four miles off," Earl said. His accent was so completely different from Theo's that I couldn't see any other kind of family resemblance between them at first. Tess and Earl's little son Daniel came running, Theo in his sights. "Dayo," he was hollering. "Uncle Dayo!" The boy crawled right up Theo's leg.

Tess and Earl had two dogs, Lola and Nashua. Lola was a Shepherd. Nashua was black as Cinder but much smaller, and somewhat frazzled from having Lola herding her around all day. The two of them taught Mingus how to be a country dog in five minutes flat. The rules were simple: pee on anything you like, dig here, dig there, run off on a whim and don't come back even if everyone's calling you, chasing you — it's fun, it's a game.

Earl walked us through a cornfield, two acres square, down to where the house was going up. So far it was only a raw wood frame, naked posts and struts, gaping holes where, one day, windows and doors would be. A year and a half now Earl had been working on it — in the summers, in the evenings, in between what paying jobs he could get.

"It's coming along all right," he said.

"Slow," said Tess.

"But it'll be a beauty." We all agreed on that.

Tess and I left Theo and Earl alone to speak in their own lingo, part English, part French, part carpentry. We headed back up through the corn to see about lunch. The camper trailer Tess and Earl had been living in the past four years was looking worse for wear. At night, Tess said, when their boy was asleep and the dogs were piled up like logs in front of the woodstove, dark sounds seeped into the trailer. Screech owls barked and chuckled. Woodlot trees talked together — branches scraping, trunks grunting. Earl and Tess lay diagonally in the trailer's too-short double bed and talked about the house.

"It'll be worth it, Tess. It'll be worth it," Earl said to her, his hands rough as spruce bark on her skin. Plans and elevations were his sweet nothings. Stone wall foundation, brace-frame construction, mortise-and-tenon joints. They were doing things the old way, the hard way.

"Authentic," was how he put it.

Anyway, they couldn't afford to go any faster.

Tess carved slabs of whole-wheat bread off a loaf still hot from the oven and sandwiched a sampling of the garden in between them. We ate outside around an unlit barbeque pit. "Our dining room," Earl said, putting his whole face into his smile. After lunch, Theo pitched his tent in the thick grass beside the cornfield. And that's right where we left him.

"You could stay for a few days," he said. "Hang out."

"There's plenty of room." Tess threw her arms wide.

"Camping's not my thing," I said.

"Guess you got enough of it," Earl said slowly. So. Theo had told him something of how I'd grown up.

"Lifetime supply," I said, relieved.

"Besides, Mingus has things to do in the city," Theo said.

"Yeah, he gets grouchy without his morning latté."

"And he has that gig at the Jazz Fest…"

Joking is the only sensible way to say good-bye.

Mingus and I drove home on the highway the whole way. He wanted as little time in the car as possible and I wanted to get us settled into a routine of some kind. Until Theo and I had moved in together I'd been wearing out my second-hand clothing and not replacing it, washing dishes as I needed them, spending days on end stepping over books and papers thematically ordered on the floor. The few pieces of furniture I owned had come from the alleyway. Theo's handmade dressers, desks and armoires made my stuff seem like crap in comparison. Some of it would have to go, but I didn't know what yet. The age difference between us didn't freak me out as much as did the disparity in our housekeeping skills.

Julie stopped in on Mingus and me a few times in between tradeshows, but otherwise we were on our own. He knew the word WALK. Even if you spelled it out. Even if you just said, "YOU WANT TO GO FOR A …?" He knew the sound of a plastic bag rustling. We walked and walked and rarely on the sidewalk. He knew every inch of every alley in Mile End by heart. I'd never really noticed the goings-on in the alleyways before Mingus came to stay. Moving-day garbage accumulated, got picked through, got rained on, got pissed on by cats and dogs and men, until eventually the city cleared it away. Kitchen gardens sent grape and zucchini vines pouring over the back fences. Peasant farmers lurked behind, barking out orders to spouses and offspring in Portuguese, Italian and Greek. Through open gates we spied tomatoes towering out of old lard buckets. Over the bird sounds, we heard the breezy clatter of aluminium pie plates hung to scare off the crows.

We noticed an inordinate number of bricks in the alleys, as if every college student in Mile End had dismantled their temporary bookshelves and moved on. I decided to rip out my rotten back porch and put in a brick walkway. Painfully aware that Theo would do a far superior job of it, I toiled to finish it before his return. Down this garden-project path I stumbled and tripped, with back bent and knees cut open. All summer long I swept and sawed and ripped and raked and shovelled and squatted and stooped and lifted and lugged and piled and sorted and fitted and filled — all to get from here to there.

Every day the bottom back step was loose and the landlord didn't fix it and neither did the upstairs neighbours and certainly neither did I.

I would wait for the sun to sink into an armchair and then I'd do the same. A place to sit in the sun and read. And a dog to go for long walks with. All that was missing was Theo. But I didn't miss him. We'd only lived together for a few months, but we lived together so well that I suspected we'd continue to do so for a very long time. I fully intended to enjoy what might be my last-ever summer of living alone.

I knew for sure that Theo and I would be together forever when his mother continued to come around to check up on me while he was away. She showed up at my door at all hours, unannounced, with bags of groceries containing useless items such as green bell peppers and cans of baby corn, asking impertinent questions such as: "*C'est a qui ça, c'est vieux manteau?*" fingering a well-worn leather jacket hanging in the hall. When I told her that was my favourite jacket, she offered to take it to a leather repair place she knew. She skirted Mingus cautiously, all the while fishing for information about Earl and her grandson, little Daniel. She was relentless. I couldn't help but like her.

At the end of our bachelor summer, Mingus and I borrowed Julie's car again and drove back down to Vermont to retrieve Theo. Mingus was somewhat more enthusiastic about the car now that he knew there was a field at the other end of it. We stopped in on our old friend, the South Hero Island Cemetery. The fork in the road at the *Drink 7-Up* store couldn't come soon enough for us. And there was the farmer's market with the homemade maple cookies, and there was the swaybacked barn in the sun on the straightaway. The dirt road had eroded to a washboard pattern that I took too fast, up, up into the high plains. Mingus was standing in the backseat by the time we heard Tess and Earl's dogs barking. It took him all of two seconds to fall back into his country dog routine.

Theo's arms, legs and back had gone nut brown from working outside.

"Why workout," he asked, "when you can work outside?"

We sat like stones around the barbecue pit, the debris of our meal strewn about us. No one said much, no one moved. The sun had almost set, the Green Mountains fading from fuchsia to blue. Out in the cornfield, the trailer glowed gold for a bit, then it dimmed too. Through the dusk and ripened cornhusks the new house hesitated, still not finished, though Theo and Earl had worked like slaves all summer, from the looks of things.

"They moved like echoes of each other," Tess said, and I could picture it: their saws wheezing, hammers blowing sharp notes out over the high plains. Tess had no time to wonder what they said to each other, in their mongrel mix of languages, up and down ladders all day, with nails in their teeth. She had her hands full chasing after little Daniel. And the dogs, when they'd take off down to the Keeler's pond. And the goats, who would climb the woodpile whenever they needed milking. And the planting, pruning, picking, washing, watering and weeding. Tess was tough enough. She'd grown up on a Montana cattle ranch. "But it was such a huge operation," she said. "Didn't seem to have anything to do with me."

"I gather homesteading was Earl's idea?"

"Forty acres doesn't seem like a lot until you start to dig it up," she said.

In the half-light of the evening things slanted out of proportion. Shadows chased across our faces. The gladiolas reared up taller than the corn. Sunburnt, barefoot and mosquito-bitten, somehow fall had crept up on all of us. Winter hung over the homestead like a debt.

Earl looked beyond his years — slumped in his lawn chair, steeped in his weariness, heavy-limbed and saw-dusted from his struggles with the house. Little Daniel sat still as well water at his father's feet. Theo had gone all boyish, sheepish; we were leaving in the morning. Back to Montreal, to his cabinetry course, to more money and more interesting, more detailed work.

The dogs were getting restless, like guests who hadn't planned to stay for dinner. Too humble to go for a stroll on their own, they were waiting for Tess to walk out with them, out along the thin dirt ribbon of the old Baxter Road.

Most nights Tess walked Lola and Nashua up to Hennessey's high pasture. You could see the whole North East Kingdom from up there. Even when it was dark you could feel it, the earth curving away from you. But Tess wasn't ready yet. She smoked a cigarette. No matter which way she held it, the smoke blew toward Earl.

They'd be one more winter in the trailer; no way Earl could finish that roof on his own. Half the rafters up, the other half hung, inverted, waiting, ready to go. Looked like they'd hang there all winter and warp out of shape under the weight of the snow.

Little Daniel clambered up into Tess's lap like he was a goat and she was a woodpile and stage-whispered somewhere just beyond her left ear:

"I'll never leave you, mummy."

His words fanned out over the barbecue pit, and filtered down through the rows of corn toward the bones of the unfinished house. Four years old and even he knew no one wanted Theo to go. Not yet. Theo gave me a look. He couldn't face Tess. He didn't dare look at Earl. He'd been registered for this cabinetry course for months now. Sure as hell wasn't going to put it off any longer, not even for Tess. Not even for Earl. He sat in his lawn chair with his work boots on, caught in the act of leaving, defiant and defeated all at once.

Daniel crawled backward out of Tess's lap, all knees and elbows. Suddenly full of wiggles and giggles he started a funny little dance on the hard dirt around the fire. The dogs perked up their ears. Earl stood up, light of limb now. He picked up Daniel, who squealed and laughed at us sideways, his comic scissor-kicking slicing the quiet night air to shreds.

Earl said to Tess: "Aw, hell, by the time he's twelve he'll be standing with his thumb out on the old Baxter Road waiting for a ride."

The Baxter Road. Ha. Tess and the dogs couldn't even get through to Hennessey's in winter. Daniel could stand out there all he wanted to, no car would come. Where Tess and Earl lived wasn't on the way to anywhere.

Earl swung Daniel around and waltzed him off toward the improvised outdoor bathtub on the other side of the trailer. The dogs scrambled to their feet and joined in. Theo started to pick up stray dishes, used bones and chewed-bald corncobs. In a fabulous balancing act, he made his way toward the trailer. From the vicinity of the bathtub all was laughing, shouts, splashes and trying-to-be-helpful dogs.

Tess stayed put. When her cigarette was done, she stubbed it out with her heel. Evenings, she kept her distance from the trailer. It was pickling time. Jam season. Jars to boil, beans to blanch, a mountain of dishes at the end. I'd always hidden, at harvest time. Made myself scarce when my mother brought the Mason jars up from the basement. "Every day I die in there," Tess said. I imagined her face red, dripping in sweat. The dogs panting outside the screen door, waiting to see how long she'd last. "Sometimes," Tess said, "I can't stand it." The cramped quarters, the scalding water and Tess all alone. "Sometimes I take the dishes outside and wash them down with the garden hose."

In winter, the only way Tess and Earl had to heat the trailer was with the woodstove. "And boy it runs hot! Sometimes we'll be sitting in there in the dead of winter, two thousand feet above sea level, twenty below, and winds fit to blow us right down the old Baxter Road. We'll have a fire on and all the windows open and we're sitting around in undershirts watching the walls sweat. And Earl says, 'If we don't get the house built before next winter, this little trailer's gonna drown in her own tears.'"

The sun was past down — behind the earth, below the trees. A breeze had started to work over the corn — to whisper in the ripe ears. Summer was as good as over. The fire down to nothing but a thin curl of smoke and a few late sparks.

Wrapped in a cloud of sopping towels and soaking bath toys, Earl and Daniel had gone off to bed. In his tent near the vegetable garden, Theo was already asleep. He was probably dreaming of us driving back to Montreal with nails in our tires, a roof beam tied to the bumper, Earl's measuring tape logging our miles, dovetails flying in formation overhead.

My legs were getting blotchy and goose-pimpled from the cool night air. Tess told me that in the morning she'd start in on the beets. Two bushels she had left, to peel and slice and pickle. We stood up, and sure enough, the dogs were under our feet, ready to carry us along. Lola and Nashua knew the way better than Tess did, in the dark. They led us through the cornfields, out to the old Baxter Road.

"Not tonight, but sometimes, I swear," Tess said, "if I thought even for a minute that there'd be any car at all anywhere for miles, I'd stick out my thumb and wait for a ride."

Tess and the dogs and I walked up toward Hennessey's. The high pasture waited for us, like a breath held in the chest.

Theo, Mingus and I left early in the morning while little Daniel was still sleeping. Tess and Earl held their dogs back so they didn't chase our car out. For miles we felt the haunt of them anyway — high plains dogs racing through the foggy dips and hollows of the old Baxter Road, never quite catching their prey. It was all old roads down to Montpellier, and not much for us to say, except good-bye to everything: good-bye used bookstore, good-bye flap-jack place that's only open on Saturdays, good-bye falling-down barn we both loved for no reason, good-bye rambling farm house we wished we lived in. Well, Theo wished. He'd never climbed an icy roof in a hurry to put out a chimney fire, or sat stranded for three dark days waiting for the snowplough to come through.

"You'd have to learn to drive, to live out here," I told him.

"I'd learn. For that house, I'd learn."

"That house would look great on Esplanade Street, across from the park," I said

We sped along the highway from Montpellier to Burlington, Mingus drooling in the backseat like some primordial swamp creature. We took the Champlain Islands route north, just so we could stop in the graveyard again. "Our graveyard." This time Mingus peed on a Baker family headstone. Theo called him Chet for the rest of the day.

"I like what you've done with the place," Theo said, surveying my rearrangement of our furniture. I hadn't managed to throw much of my clutter out, but I had filed most of it inside Theo's desks and dressers. I showed Theo the garden path I'd built. He promptly fixed the bottom back step.

The hardest part of having Mingus all summer was giving him back to Julie at the end of it. Once the tradeshows were all done and she was home again, she missed him. We walked him over to her place. We missed him as soon as we shut her door behind us. The way he and the bathtub rubber ducky hung out together, the way he sprawled on his stomach on the kitchen floor, hind legs flat out behind him like frogs legs. "You can still borrow him whenever you want," Julie said. But by now I knew that borrowing a dog was not the same as living with one. Theo had spent all summer with Tess and Earl's dogs, Lola and Nashua, and he was missing them too. I'd just read Arundhati Roy's novel *The God of Small Things*. Mingus was the Dog of Small Things. When he left, he left a Mingus-shaped hole in the universe. A hole that eerily resembled a new water stain spreading on the kitchen ceiling.

Our upstairs neighbour said we should thank our landlord for providing such affordable slum housing. I wrote the landlord terse letters:

Dear Mister G:

The kitchen ceiling is now officially falling down in three places. The water stain directly below the upstairs neighbour's bathtub continues to grow. Yesterday it sprung a leak. The neighbour assures me that he does not regularly allow his bathtub to overflow, as you suggest. He also informs me that you recently repaired a leak in the copper pipes leading to his bathtub with silicone caulking. We both feel that soldering the pipes would have been more effective! Speaking of plumbing, let me remind you for the third time now that the hot water heater can no longer heat enough water to fill our bathtub. We cannot continue taking shallow baths into the winter. Speaking of heating, the kitchen stove is now down to one burner and must be replaced. Please advise, Simone.

Not going back to school in the fall felt downright unnatural. I'd gobbled up my degree (like a weak child, starved for food.) Now it was finished and I had the bill to pay. I missed my old job at the university library and had no idea how to find new work. Theo decided we needed a computer. He'd use it to keep track of his business and I'd use the Internet to search for work. After three weeks of thorough research he decided on the exact make and model. The computer was a grey-beige box. The monitor, a beetle-black glass eye. Cables snaked away from its hindquarters. The contraption was by far the ugliest thing in our apartment. It did everything Theo told it to do and wouldn't listen to me at all. This just goaded me on. I spent the rest of the fall trying to master its inner workings.

"This machine hates me," I complained.

"Stand your ground," Theo said. "They can smell fear."

"That's not fear it's smoke — open up the flue a bit." Theo put our first woodstove fire of the season out instead, took down all the stovepipes and cleaned out the creosote. That's how he does things. All or nothing. The next fire did burn better. But then the computer froze on me.

"Now look what you've done," I said. "All that attention you paid to the woodstove made the computer jealous."

I figured out how to use the Internet to buy a plane ticket to Nova Scotia. I don't know why I decided to visit my parents, or why I thought winter was the time to do it. A winter when I was in debt, full of doubt and everything outside was already dark and mean. But ever since the one night we'd spent in Theo's tent at the edge of his half-brother's cornfield, the wind across the high plains, the pickled beets Tess had sent us home with I'd had some kind of craving. Not to return, only to visit.

"A fact-finding mission," I called it.

"A guilt trip," Theo suggested.

"It's all your brother's fault," I said.

"That's my mother's line."

The flight from Montreal to Halifax wasn't long enough for the passengers to settle properly. We sat high in our seats, buoyant. I had never flown before. I kept my forehead pressed to the cool, oval, airplane window, even though it was night. On our approach to Halifax, tiny lights poked through the dark nothing.

From the air, the lights on the ground resembled stars. We flew toward them — the heavens growing nearer, brighter. The night sky inverted, perverted, projected patterns upon the black earth screen. Highways sliced through forest. Strip malls clustered like bright pustules. The porches and streetlights of swirling sub-divisions made new constellations, their names unknown to me.

From the height of the escalator, I spotted my father — a dark, brooding Rembrandt in the otherwise fair-haired crowd. The meagre terminal building was aggressively lit, fluorescent to fight off the early-evening darkness. Holiday-garish garlands decked the luggage carousels, temporary talismans against the chill Maritime air. Freshly-scrubbed family members waited to engulf their newly returned loved ones in the home-again smell of wet wool coats. Jostled by the eager elbows of returning students waiting cousins and children running about, bankers and farmers, wives and fishermen — all decked in their holiday-best outfits — I headed toward my father. He stood alone, further back, half hidden by a pillar. I recognized the smell of his parka, encrusted with the working dust of the barn, the dust that came from the thick winter fur of the animals, from rubbing against them, from feeding them twice a day. All the people seemed as horses, tossing their heads and laughing with the excitement of the holiday ahead. They stomped their feet and shifted their weight beside the luggage carousels and when their suitcases came they lifted them gaily like fragrant bales of hay.

I followed my father in silence to the elevator and rode down with him to the parking level. His boots shed small, dried chunks of manure. The other passengers delicately sidestepped these. Herded by family, they headed toward their cars.

Ours was not the only pick-up in the parking lot, but it was the meanest looking one — dented and dirty with two bales of hay in the back for weight, for traction. Once we were seatbelted in my father said, "One of the Jersey heifers is half dead, from what, we don't know yet." He manoeuvred out of the parking space with accusatory precision and made his way toward the exit with stealth. "Your mother is there with the vet," he said as he paid the parking attendant. "Your mother," he said, as he navigated his way onto the two and a half hours of highway ahead of us, "has got to learn to drive."

"She knows how to drive."

"Yes, but she won't."

The Jersey wasn't half dead, not even a quarter. Everything was fine. Well, not fine exactly, but the same. Well, not quite the same, but consistent with how it had been in the past. My mother had gone from plump to fat, which somehow made her look younger. She was well into the third book in a series of historical mystery novels set during the Punic wars. Historical? Mystery? Novels? My God. My father still looked solid as a cast-iron skillet but now moved heavy as one too. He could barely get through a page of the Atlantic Monthly before falling asleep on the couch. Periodicals? I'd brought the wrong gifts. I'd packed the wrong clothes. I'd prepared answers to questions that were never asked.

"How's Isaac?" I asked.

"Who?" My father woke with a start.

"Isaac."

"How should I know?"

"Navy," my mother said.

"You're joking."

"Nope."

"Why didn't you tell me?"

"You didn't ask."

"I've asked about him every time I've phoned."

"And we told you. He's fine. He just happens to be in the Navy."

"How are the Vaughns?" I asked. "Have any of them joined the Navy?"

"Go ask them yourself," my father said, from which I gathered they still lived down the road.

I went out to the barn. Red, at least, was happy to see me. I saddled him up, old as he was now, cold as it was out. The wander down the Sloane Road to the Vaughn place seemed shorter. From out in the driveway we could hear little kids screaming. Maybe the Vaughn trailer was haunted now. Maybe we were all still in there — Jack Junior and his sisters and me — playing jacks, reading Archie Digests, eating sugar and watching TV. I knocked, and then felt like an idiot. I'd never knocked at the Vaughns' before. A hulking young woman yanked the door open. I stared at her dumbly. She had a baby under one arm and a patch of angry, red eczema under one eye. My parents would have told me, wouldn't they, if the Vaughns had moved away?

"Simone, is that you?"

I blinked.

"It's me, Jeanie," she said. "Come on in."

Neither Jeanie Vaughn nor the Vaughn trailer had aged well. Jeanie was only two years older than me. While I'd been getting a degree in Art History, she'd been popping out babies. At least three. "And counting," as my mother used to say of Jeanie's parents. "How are your parents?" I asked. An excruciating half-hour account of who was doing what then ensued. I could only follow bits and pieces of it. Names that must have been well known to me were no longer familiar. Relationships once clear to me were now confused.

"Where's Jack at?" I asked. One day back on the Sloane Road and already my grammar had gone to hell.

"Which Jack?" Jeanie wanted to know.

Our Jack, I almost said. "Your brother."

"He's a baker now."

"A baker?" The Montrealer in me struggled to envision Jack Vaughn concocting croissants, éclairs and tartelettes. Vachon cakes seemed more his speed.

"Yeah, at the Tim's out by the Michelin Plant. He has a kid too."

"Named Jack?"

"We call him Jack Rabbit."

Whether Jack had a wife or not, or if Jeanie had a husband, I never determined.

"You still look like Veronica," she told me as I stood to go. There wasn't a shred of Betty left in her.

Theo called me my last night in Nova Scotia to warn me. "Take a taxi from the airport, I'll pay for it." There'd been a big storm in Montreal. He didn't want his mother driving. "The roads are treacherous enough with her on them, forget about the ice."

I knew in the truck with my father driving down the bitter highway toward the airport that I would never try to visit the farm again — not for summers nor birthdays nor the pale imitations of holidays we didn't celebrate anyway. No more summers walking with Red as far away from the house as I could get, hiding in the ruins of the long-ago house of some other family, reading histories that could never be mine. No more bleak Decembers spent chilled by my father's indifference, exasperated by my mother's deferrals — to me, to him. "Which do *you* prefer?" I'd asked at last and got no answer. We'd sat with our backs turned to the fire, faces turned from each other. There was no more cold comfort in the wall of books. I'd read all of them, and many more besides.

It wasn't until we landed in Montreal that I discovered just how bad the storm had been. The roads were fine, but the wreckage from high winds and heavy snow remained. The Congolese taxi driver was intrepid, considering he was braving his first Canadian winter. "Normal? Normal?" he kept asking, incredulous at the sheer size of the snow removal vehicles. We inched past an overturned tractor-trailer on the 40. "Normal?"

"Wind," I said, craning for some sign that this wasn't Isaac's dad's truck. Why hadn't I thought to ask if he was still driving long haul?

"Normal?" the taxi driver asked of a massive tree down on Waverly Street.

"Let me out here," I said, and dragged my suitcase into the *ruelle*. Our power was out, our pipes had frozen in the night, the hot water heater had burst and there was water all over the kitchen floor. We had enough faith in our landlord to know that we wouldn't see hot water again for at least five days.

"Why didn't you tell me this on the phone?" I asked Theo.

"What would you have done about it?"

This is someone you spend the rest of your life with, someone who knows what not to tell you on the phone.

We decided we had to move. And fast. We barely had to hunt for a new apartment because as soon as we'd made up our minds an *À Louer* sign appeared on a second floor place on Saint-Urbain Street, right around the corner.

"I like how we noticed the sign because the sun was shining directly on it."

"A good sign."

We went to take a look. Not only was the apartment sunny, it was so warm inside we had to take off our coats. There were hardly any cracks in the walls at all. The high ceilings were falling down in zero places and the rooms were huge. The couple living there were about to have a baby. They wanted out as soon as possible. Our landlord agreed to let us out of our lease early. He was more than happy to get rid of us. All we'd done was complain. With us gone he could raise the rent by at least fifty bucks a month. He'd find someone, soon enough, to fall for the rustic charm of the place, some romantic with no idea what work it is to heat with wood. We didn't have to wait until the first of July to move, but we did have to wait for the worst of the spring slush and dog shit to wash away. We didn't bother to rent a truck. We just carried stuff over. A hundred times we stood on the west side of Saint-Urbain Street holding something preposterous — a rubber tree, a ceiling fan, all our coats slumped over one arm, a lamp in each hand — waiting for a break in the traffic so we could cross the street.

By mid-May we were settled in. I set up a home office in the back room where the bedroom would normally be. I upgraded the computer and set about teaching myself HTML. We put our bed in the smaller section of the *salon double*. A rounded archway divided the room. There were pillars at either end of the arch, with plinths with cupids on them.

"This place is a classic!" Adrian shrieked when he saw the cupids. The less we saw of him the more over-the-top he seemed. The more over-the-top he seemed the more sense he made, so we did our best to see less and less of him.

"Mais il n'y a pas de place pours un lave-vaisselle?" Theo's mother said, as forcibly well intentioned as ever.

We soon discovered that our new apartment was hot as hell in the summer without both the front and back doors open. Like most Montreal apartments, we had two balconies: one on the street, front, and one in the back alley, rear. The front balcony was black metal, a sun-hot and traffic-loud square. The back balcony was larger, wooden — quieter. We used it as an extra room, a slim

slice of outdoors, a place to hang laundry, fix bicycles, pot plants and store such ungainly household items as step-ladders, mops and brooms. Of course, everybody else used their back balconies this way too, each one a stage upon which family dramas unfolded, from which lovelorn orations were issued. Clotheslines reeled in and out between the acts.

In this intimacy born of proximity, our nearest neighbour and I went about our business. Theo and I called her the Old Greek Lady. Foul-mouthed for seventy, her first-floor curses filled our second-floor apartment; her constant commentary punctuated my day.

"Fuck you!" she hollered as she handed laundry to her silent husband. He grimly reeled out each day's garments, clothesline low over scarecrowed tomatoes.

I envied them their garden.

Always civil, the Old Greek Lady and I waved to each other. To each her own. Undies, bedsheets, and bras danced on the line — a curtain of delicates to separate her balcony from mine.

From my home office window, I watched the comings and goings of a crew of alley cats. The way they studiously avoided one another made me suspect they were all relatives. They slid under fences and up back steps, dug in gardens and clawed at garbage bags out back. Sometimes late at night we'd hear them caterwauling, scuffling and fighting in brief moments of feral love. These cats made our old barn cats look like pussycats, as it were. The alley cats could kick the barn cats' asses.

A band of children also roamed the alley. The alley kids, we called them. They were less adventurous, more domesticated. They wore their helmets when they rode their bikes, and came when they were called. Our landlord / downstairs neighbour's grandchildren were another story. The Infestation, we called them. Much to our horror, not long after we moved in, our landlord installed an aboveground pool in the back yard, and donned a Speedo. His wife was fat, and all five of their grandchildren were screamers. Amusement-park loud and B-movie shrill. We soon wearied of writing out rent cheques to a man of whom we saw so much hairy flesh.

"He should be paying us," Theo felt.

"Worker's compensation," I agreed. How was I going to get anything done, with child noise and hard, white light bouncing off chemical-bright water flooding my office window?

One of my favourite things about Theo was that he wanted kids even less than I did. I don't mind kids, in theory. I'm pretty good with children in fact. It's people I'm related to that I have a problem with. Reproducing my parents, or Theo's, was a risk we weren't willing to take. But what about a dog? Would I hate it if it took after me? Skinny, runty, talks-too-much? What were the chances of it taking after Theo? Calm, patient and stubborn? I decided: if and when Theo made up his mind that we could do it, then we could do it. Theo is about the only person on the planet who can successfully say no to me. So when he says yes, I believe it.

69

Don't even walk into the SPCA unless you mean it. Know what you want before you go in. Or tell yourself you do. It helps if you have an hour's ride on the Metro to psych yourself up. "There'll be no sleeping on the bed," I said. "Not even once. Let him get away with something once and that's it, he'll do it again and again."

"We just have to be consistent, that's all," Theo said.

"Yeah, like we are in real life."

"Ha ha ha."

Talk it over all you want — purebred dogs versus mutts, female versus male — when you get to the Namur Metro station all bets are off. Walk toward the SPCA, and you can hear the dogs barking from out on the street. Walk through those doors and you enter a process of unnatural selection, evolution turned on its ear by the abuse, neglect and capricious whims of humans. The noise and smell, combined with the guilt and fear of making a wrong decision, one with long-term consequences, really brings out the shallow in a person. We wanted a dog a little bit like Mingus because we missed him, but not too much because then we'd always be making comparisons with him. We wanted a young dog — as yet undamaged by previous owners. If anyone was going to mess up our dog, it was going to be us.

The day we went to the SPCA, all the dogs were fully-grown and none of them looked even remotely like Mingus. We toured the room slowly. Dogs leapt at us as we passed, hurling themselves at the metal bars of their kennels, barking their heads off.

"Seriously, I think that Shepherd is going to actually bark its own head off."

All barking and all fully-grown except for one small, black-and-white creature curled up in a tight knot as far back in the kennel as it could get. Male, according to the tag on the kennel door. Abandoned. And asleep.

"How can he sleep, with all this noise?" I asked. At the sound of my voice he opened one eye to take a look at us.

"Hi," we said. He sighed, an old man sigh, as if we were disturbing him from a much needed post-shuffleboard tournament snooze. He stood up reluctantly, as if he'd been through this routine a number of times already. He shook himself awake and slowly walked to the front of the kennel. He was a scrawny thing, with impossibly large floppy ears. He wore a white tuxedo-front stomach, and mismatched white socks on his feet.

"What kind of dog do you think he is?" Theo asked. The tag on his kennel said he was a four-month-old Lab-Border Collie mix, but that barely seemed plausible.

"I don't know. He kind of looks like a cartoon character."

"From an old black-and-white cartoon."

"Did Betty Boop have a butler?"

We squatted down in front of his kennel to get a better look at him. He sat down too, like he was exhausted. He probably was. The tag said he'd been at the SPCA a week already. A week with all that barking. I put my hand out for him to sniff. He sniffed. And then he stuck a front paw out between the bars and, well, pawed my hand with it.

"He's shaking my hand!"

"I think you two have just made an agreement of some kind," Theo said. The dog turned and looked at him. He had tiny white dots above each eye that moved up and down when he blinked. He looked back at me, and cocked his head to one side in what could only be described as a full-body question mark.

"You do that," Theo said.

"What?"

"You tilt your head like that sometimes, when you're asking a question."

"Oh, man, we're done for," I said.

There was an awful lot of paperwork to fill out, for such a little dog. And then yet more decisions to make: what food to buy, what leash, what collar.

"You'd think a collar would come standard."

"He's equipped with four-wheel drive, but air-conditioning is extra."

We had to call Theo's mother to get a lift back to our place. Our new best friend, the cartoon character, kept up his demure act until the moment we got him outside. And then Mr. Hyde-like, he turned into a wild animal, sniffing at everything, paying no attention to us, trying to run in every direction but getting nowhere, straining at his brand-new leash. We stood on a shabby patch of grass beside the SPCA, waiting for Theo's mother, watching this spectacle, sceptical. Theo, the eternally calm, was studying the dog's antics intently, as if some kind of pattern could be discerned from them. I was taking a considerably less reflective approach.

"What have we done?" I wailed.

Theo's mother was not impressed with us, not one bit. The dog was not helping. The little monster writhed in my lap, squeaking and kicking and stinking of fear, old piss and kennel in the backseat of Theo's mother's immaculate car. Theo sat up front and spoke quiet French to her, as if that would somehow distract her from the smell. She lectured him: dogs are dirty, dogs are noisy, dogs are a lot of work.

"*Ma*," Theo kept saying.

"*SIT*," I kept saying to the dog, with equal futility. At some point I realized that Thérèse was telling me the story of Tasha over her shoulder while she drove. I'd heard different versions of this story already, in both English and French. Theo and Earl had had a Beagle named Tasha when Theo was about six and Earl was fourteen. Tasha had only lasted for a few months before Thérèse sent her packing. The rest of the family agreed that the reason they'd had to get rid of Tasha was because she bit Theo in the ass. Theo remembers it differently, of course. In his version, yes, she bit him, but just a nip. They were just playing, an elaborate game that no one else understood. In his version he and Tasha were best friends. But, speeding down Côte Sainte-Catherine, his mother was sticking to the story she'd made up twenty-five years ago to get rid of the dog in the first place.

"*Oui, je connais l'histoire,*" I said, but there was no stopping her. The dog, however, stopped writhing for a second to look at me funny. Who knows, I thought, maybe he was fluent in French. "*Doucement!*" I'd heard Julie say to Mingus. I gave it a try, but nothing doing. He went back to his infernal squirming, kicking me in the stomach, trying to climb up me like he was a demented mountain goat.

Thérèse screeched to a halt in front of our place. She couldn't wait to get the stinking, deluded lot of us out of her car. The second I put the dog down on the sidewalk he attempted to make a break for it, pulling at the leash with all of his ten pounds. Sheer force of will. Theo had some terse words in French with his mother through her car window and finally she was off, swerving into the Saint-Urbain Street traffic without signalling, eliciting a cacophony of screeching tires, car horns and curses. We turned our backs to the street. We don't know that lady. Nope, nothing to do with us, no sir.

"UP," we said encouragingly, pointing at the front steps, making up-type gestures with our hands. The little dog looked at us like we were talking crazy talk. From his point of view, which was less than one foot off the ground, our front steps looked like a ladder — horizontal lines with nothing in between them. How the hell was he supposed to know what was up top? Maybe nothing, maybe a cage, maybe yet another kennel full of piss and grown dogs barking. Finally we consented to carry him up the front steps, but once we were inside we put him down again right away because Theo had read somewhere that carrying your dog around is one of the best ways to make it stupid.

The first thing our new dog did inside our apartment was pee on a pile of shoes by the door. "So it's going to be like that is it?" We carried him back down the steps for an emergency walk around the block. The leash was a torment to him — he strained against it, pulling, fighting, and flailing in every direction. The heap of garbage outside the empanada place on the corner was a gold mine, to his mind — it took our full strength to drag him past it. In the alley we prayed he'd pee while still tethered. We didn't dare let him off leash in this feral state. He'd forget we existed in seconds. All he could think about was scavenging for food.

What he considered food was alarming. Suddenly we saw the alley as a minefield of potentially ingestible items: a bagel as big as his head, a pizza crust, a chicken bone, a plate of soggy cat food, a rotten apple, the feathered breast of something dead.

"We have food for you at home, you little freak," we told him, our hands in his mouth fishing after each new half-chewed horror.

"Good dog!" we gushed as, at long last, he deposited a turd for us to pick up.

"You can do it," we told him as he stared sceptically up at our front stairs again.

"You need a bath," Theo informed him.

"Good luck with that," I said and left the two of them to duke it out *mano a mano* in the bathroom. We'd had the dog for all of forty-seven minutes and I was already exhausted. After the bath we fed him. His whole head disappeared inside the food bowl. After the food we walked him again. After the walk he needed a nap. After every nap he had to pee again. After changing his mind he had to pee again. In between naps and walks he trotted around the apartment sniffing out our life stories.

"He's casing the joint."

"Looking for escape routes."

"Looking for a safe place to sleep."

I built a bed for him out of a pillowcase and some old mattress foam that Theo had tried to convince me we no longer had any use for back when we were packing up to move. As soon as I set this pillowcase mattress foam pallet down on the floor our wild dog knew what it was for. He walked across the room toward it, flopped himself down onto it and claimed it as his own.

"See, I *knew* we'd need this foam for something!"

"All right, all right." Theo set about making us gigantic cocktails, which we were much in need of. We wound up drinking them out in the alley because by then, of course, the dog needed to pee again.

"Do you think this makes us bad parents?" I asked, vodka in one hand, poop bag in the other.

"I just hope he'll sleep through the night."

So far, I loved him most when he was asleep.

After a few days of trial and mostly error, I was convinced we were doing everything as wrong as possible. We yelled our heads off at the little creep — NO SIT DOWN STAY — and he didn't listen to single a thing we said. We couldn't even come up with a name. We'd tried lots of different ones but none seemed right.

"How about Jackass?" Theo said, his considerable patience wearing thin.

"How about Asshole?" I said. "All he does is shit."

I feared that every mistake we made now would haunt us for the rest of our dog's life. I called up Julie and begged her to come over.

"I need a reality check," I said.

"I'm sure you're doing a great job," she said, but I insisted.

"I'm now thoroughly housebroken, but the dog's still a jerk."

Julie and I walked the dog around the corner to the alley; a battle of wills the whole way. I kept yanking guiltily at the medieval-looking choke chain we'd inherited from a Black Lab owner up the street who'd seen our back alley struggles and insisted that a tug on the choke chain followed by a stern "Heel," every single time he pulled on the leash was the only thing that would work. As it was, I was yanking and yelling, "Heel," every ten seconds and the dog was still straining hard as ever to escape.

"He'd rather strangle himself than listen to me!"

"I wouldn't take it personally," Julie said. "All dogs pull at first."

"Even Mingus?"

"Are you kidding? He was a total bastard for the whole first year I had him."

"Wait, is that supposed to make me feel better or worse?"

We got halfway down the alley before I would admit that I was afraid to let him off the leash. "What if he doesn't come back?"

"Say his name," Julie said.

"ISAAC," I said to the dog. And it worked! The dog looked up at me.

"You're gonna be fine," Julie said.

"You're sure you don't mind?" I prodded Theo, when he got home that evening. I had told him, of course, about Isaac the boy, my only friend besides the horse. But this dog was both of ours. I wasn't sure about naming him after someone Theo never knew.

Theo looked down at the dog, who was sniffing the refrigerator door intently, convinced there was food in there but unsure, yet, how to get at it. "Isaac," Theo said. The dog looked up at him. Theo laughed. "What can I say — Isaac appears to be this dog's name."

Isaac feigned complete indifference to us when we were both at home, but then the minute either one of us even looked toward the front door he started whining and yawing accusatorily. While Theo was out at work, Isaac and I were fused together in tense symbiosis. He followed me from room to room. Even to the bathroom. I tried to teach him the word *privacy*, to no avail. Every little sound made his ears twitch. When he finally did fall asleep, I stayed put, sitting as still as possible so as not to wake him. Because the minute he woke I'd have to take him out to pee again. I got lots of work done this way. By way of avoiding walking the dog a hundred times a day I conquered the computer. And the Internet. HTML was now powerless to resist me. JavaScript would soon be within reach.

The minute the dog woke up we'd be out in the alley again. My neck became sore from looking down at him constantly. I memorized every crack in the pavement, every puddle, drainage grate, speed bump, cat-food-danger-spot and broken-glass-zone. Weeks passed before I was able to look up at anything taller than the dog: weeds, wild flowers, raspberry bushes. It took months for the social complexities of our back alley to really sink in.

Mingus and I had studied the alleyways intersecting Groll Street. Since Theo and I had moved to the other side of Saint-Urbain Street those alleys seemed miles away. Our new alley was not the nicest in the neighbourhood, but it wasn't the worst one either. Kitchen gardens and garbage heaps coexisted. Wildflowers thrived amidst the dog shit. Graffiti, zucchini and grapevines all vied for attention. Hand-painted signs warned: *défense déchets, défense de stationner*. Stray cats, cooking smells and laundry lines crisscrossed the alleyways one sentence at a time. Daily, the dog and I walked through this interior city, sniffing for stories.

Whenever possible, Theo and I walked Isaac together, comparing notes constantly, in an effort to ensure that we were each teaching him the same rules. We kept an eagle eye out for other dogs, suspiciously at first, fearing that Isaac would run across the street to talk to one. Gradually we sought them out, hoping to socialize Isaac. Soon we knew most of the other dogs in the neighbourhood by name. At home, we talked about them as if they were people.

"For the first year or so dogs and babies are exactly alike," a new friend from the dog park informed me. She had one of each. To test this theory I sent a ball rolling down her hallway. Her kid went crawling after it, caught up with it, and put it in his mouth.

Tosca was a Great Dane so large Isaac trembled when he saw her; he crouched down on the pavement or leaned against my leg. Cartier was bred by the Mira Foundation to be a seeing-eye dog. She didn't make the cut, but many of her puppies did. Doctor didn't want to bark when we walked past his backyard, but he couldn't help it. "Doctor," someone from somewhere inside his apartment hollered and just like that all Doctor's barks stopped. Gimlet was a tiny grey thing at the end of a very long leash, a busybody, a social commentator. When it snowed, Gimlet barked at the flakes, telling them: "Hey, knock it off. Hey, that's enough. Hey, I can't walk in this — I'm too short. You're burying me!" When he saw Isaac on the sidewalk, he barked at him, telling him: "Hey, I know you. Hey, you're getting big. Hey, guess what I did today?" Bella was a tiny dog who we worried would get squashed to death because her mom's boyfriend was a dead-beat. Rage was a gigantic Newfoundland. Despite his daunting size, unfortunate name, and tendency to drool, Rage was one of Isaac's favourite dog park friends.

Isaac, it appeared, had a bias toward black dogs. He developed a crush on a little Black Lab named Zig-Zig about a year-and-a-half older than him. At first we thought Zig-Zig was named for her running style. When every other dog in the pack zigged, Zig-Zig zagged. Just like in *The Phantom Tollbooth* when Tock, the watchdog, actually went Tick. "Be your own dog, Zig-Zig," her mother would positively reinforce her. One day we were in the park with Zig-Zig and her mom, and a guy showed up with a dog named Sputnik.

"It's the reunion tour!" Zig-Zig's mom shouted.

"They know each other?" I asked.

"Zig-Zig Sputnik is a punk rock band," Theo explained. How did he know these things? I was sick of being the least punk rock person I knew.

Mingus completely ignored Isaac, which took a lot of effort on his part as Isaac pulled out his full arsenal of puppy tricks to try and get Mingus to chase, play, and fight with him. Mingus hid under the kitchen table. Julie and I drank iced tea.

"Is Mingus offended that I'm cheating on him with another dog?"

"Nah," Julie assured me. "Isaac's energy just makes him feel old."

"Mingus is an old soul."

"Plus, I think Isaac is too young to really appreciate jazz."

By fall we'd fallen into the same dog-walking schedule as a couple from the Maritimes named Wallace and Dee. Theo thought these names were hilarious. I assured him they were as common as Lion and Bright.

"Who are Lion and Bright?"

"Oxen. In Nova Scotia, all team oxen are named Lion and Bright."

Theo didn't believe me, which made me doubt myself for a second.

"Ask Wallace and Dee," I said. Theo wouldn't, convinced I was pulling his leg. So the next time we saw them, I asked them, and Wallace confirmed it. "Sure enough," he said, laying the accent on thick. Finally, folks who knew exactly where I'd come from. Why had I never thought to befriend expatriates before?

Wallace was a big guy, with a lumbering gait. Polo shirts, khakis and deck shoes were all we ever saw him in. Dee was shorter, but not by much, a solid plump with a penchant for floral-print blouses and gigantic hair clips. Wallace and Dee's dog's name was Box. They got questions about it, they said, but no, Box was not a Boxer. Not even close. More like a beige Whippet mixed with something spotty. Wallace had found him in a cardboard box on the side of the road. They tried calling him Rex, but it didn't stick. They bought him a padded basket to sleep in, but Box had a thing for cardboard. Some dogs pick their own names.

Wallace taught science in an otherwise all-arts high school. Dee worked part-time in the library at the École Enfant Jésus. Their jobs had little in common besides the long summer vacations. For years now, they'd summered on the Grand Manan. End of June they packed up their car, put Box in a half-a-box basket in the backseat and drove until they hit the water. The ferry from Blacks Harbour only ran once a day. They had to time it just right, but didn't quite. They left home plenty early but made too many stops along the way. Box needed bathroom breaks when Wallace and Dee didn't and vice versa. Wallace preferred the old road. But then Dee wanted to stop at all the farmers' markets and fruit stands and there were quite number of them along the way. The backseat slowly filled with salad fixings. Pints of berries spilled. Box tested the rhubarb pie.

Missing the ferry cost them an over-priced night at the Tide's Inn, where the mattresses were as lumpy as life jackets and the dining room smelled like it looked, like lacquered buoys drowning in fishing nets. But the lobster bisque wasn't too bad. And the service was personable. Box was allowed to sleep under the dinner table. By now the owner knew Wallace, Dee and Box by name.

Crossing the Bay of Fundy on the ferry the next day, Wallace and Dee promptly forgot whose fault it was that they were one day late for summer once again. Revelling in the salt wind and stiff chop, each strained to be the first to sight the island. They lived for those summers on the Grand Manan. They rented the same cottage every year. By the time they unpacked their car they'd met everyone on the island.

"Everyone and their dog," Wallace said.

"Sounds great," I said, but I could barely imagine it. I'd never been on a real vacation before, the kind where you go sit on a beach somewhere. I was much more preoccupied with finding work in the city. Theo had more work than he knew what to do with. All of a sudden people who had rented for years were buying up places. Theo and I discussed doing the same, but I didn't see how we could afford it. He still had some student loan debt to pay; I had all of mine left and was barely working. At least, we reasoned, this left me with plenty of time to raise the dog.

Isaac paced the apartment, toenails clicking on the hardwood floors. He whined at the front door. He knew there was no one there. He just wanted to lie in the pool of sun in the landing. But I couldn't open the front door for him until the mailman came. They won't deliver if there's an unleashed dog sitting in the doorway, even if the dog looks like a cartoon character. When the mail finally came I opened the front door for Isaac so he could go bake his brains out on the front balcony — black dog on black metal.

Theo did the early morning walks and then rushed off to spend the day in other people's kitchens and bathrooms. On the nights he stayed late at the wood shop working on orders for custom furniture pieces, I did the evening walk to the park; otherwise, I did the night walk. The Civilized Walk, we called it. No sticks, no balls, no games. Just pissing and sniffing, pissing and sniffing, up one side of Waverly and down the other. Every night Isaac and I walked past the Berlin restaurant at Fairmount and Saint-Urbain. One night we were standing there, waiting for the light to change, when two old guys came out of Berlin clutching brown paper doggie bags. Both of the men were red-faced and jovial, full of sausage and Schlitz.

"What's your dog's name?" they wanted to know.

"Isaac."

"Isaac? Hey Abe, this dog's Jewish! Give this dog some schnitzel."

Berlin's gone now. The wall has fallen, as it were. And what do we care? All those times we walked by we never once stopped to read the menu. A new place opened up, with fake tin ceilings, posh, dark-wood panelling and ivory, cloth-covered chairs. The dog would piss on the side of the building all the same. Every time we stood waiting for the light to change I thought: *Hey Abe, give this dog some schnitzel.*

There was a Hasidic boys' school a few doors up from the former Berlin, right between the Mikva and the Buddhist Centre. Whatever you do, don't tell the *yeshiva bokhers* that this dog's name is Isaac. They're pathologically afraid of dogs. Sure, the Cossacks used dogs to flush Jews out of ghettoes and shetels during the pogroms. But this is Mile End already. And our dog looked more and more like a cartoon character with each passing day, all long legs and floppy ears. How could it be safer to run out into Saint-Urbain Street traffic to avoid him than to pass him politely on the sidewalk? When we walked up the back alley behind the *yeshiva* at lunchtime, the boys in the windows would start yelling: "What's your dog's name? What's your dog's name?" A singsong chanting honed by years of communal praying so persistent that it was hard not to answer. Don't say Isaac. They'll taunt. He'll freak. Say Yitzhak. It's technically true. They could hang out their classroom windows and chant: "Yitzhak, Yitzhak, Yitzhak," all they wanted. Isaac wouldn't know it had anything to do with him.

"What's your dog's name?" was the first question most non-dog-owners asked. They weren't interested in the dog; they wanted to talk to me. A dog owner wanted to know: How old? What sex? What breed? What's that rash, limp, bump, bald spot? A non-dog-owner had other things on the brain. Hitting on me. Or telling me story, having a flashback, or a fantasy. They'd always wanted a dog. They had a dog like that when they were a kid. They had an ex who had a dog like that. So they asked: "What's you're dog's name?"

And when we'd tell that our dog's name was Isaac, a guessing game ensued.

"Isaac Hayes?"

"Isaac Newton?"

"Sure, kind of." There was no point in trying to explain how Isaac had picked his own name, plucked it right out of my head. How there was this boy I knew, back in Nova Scotia, how we used to trade sneakers for boots before first bell. How we played playground games and worked the haying crews together. How, somehow, I had lost touch with him. The Navy? Damn.

I now owned three pairs of cowboy boots. Every time I pulled one on Isaac the dog came running. Boots were one sure sign that I was leaving the apartment. Maybe he'd get to come with me, and maybe, and maybe! The dog's eternal optimism. Other sure signs I would soon be leaving the apartment included: socks, jeans, and mascara. The dog detested mascara. If I was putting on mascara, he knew that wherever I was going it was highly unlikely that he'd get to come with me. Every time Theo or I left the apartment we'd tell the dog: "We'll be right back." No matter how long we'd be gone.

Isaac was a mix of at least three kinds of work dog, as far as we could figure: Black Lab, German Pointer and Border Collie. Labradors are retrievers, so when we threw the ball he went after it. And German Pointers are, well, pointers. So when he caught the ball he brought it back to us, and, after giving it a good shake to make sure it was dead, he'd DROP the ball and then point at it until we picked it up and threw it again. Border Collies are smarter than all of us. This saved us a lot of time and energy. If Isaac's ball rolled under one end of the couch he'd go over to the other end and wait for it to roll out. He figured out how the slope on the kitchen floor worked, so he could play ball by himself, if he had to. More often than not he applied his considerable corralling skills toward roping us into playing with him.

"WHERE'S YOUR BALL?" we'd ask him, when it was time to go out, and he'd go find his ball, wherever it might be hiding in the apartment. "NOT THAT BALL," we'd tell him, if he brought the wrong ball, and off he'd go again until he found the right one.

Theo, Isaac and I all agreed that the best balls for playing in the alley were the orange street hockey balls that we purchased at the dollar store half a dozen at a time, in case of loss or thievery. Every now and then Isaac would find a filthy tennis ball in the alley, fall in love, drop his orange ball, and insist on bringing this new find home with him. Our apartment soon became an obstacle course of lost-and-found orange hockey balls and yellow tennis balls of varying states of disrepair.

"NO BALL," we'd tell him, if we had business to attend to on our walk. No matter. If he didn't have a ball, he'd find a stick. If he found a stick, and then found a better one, he might drop the first one, but why not try and carry both?

"Our dog has a master plan for the rearrangement of every stick in every alleyway in Mile End," Theo said.

"I know, it makes me nervous."

The bigger the stick the more Isaac liked it. If it was a fallen branch, well, then, all the better. If it had trailing leaves he'd sweep the alley clean. If it was a two-by-four two feet long or more, well, then, he'd prance out onto Saint-Viateur Street with it — head high — and whack the legs of passers-by, smack in the calves, watching them marvel at him, watching them laugh, which made us laugh. The best sticks made their way back to our place. DROP. We made him leave them outside on the front balcony, which soon resembled a bird's nest.

"I think the dog has a better work ethic than I do," I fretted to Theo. I was writing an art review here and there, and getting pretty handy with HTML. Enough to land a few web-design contracts. Those at least paid well. Not enough to pay off my student loan, not enough to keep the dog in kibble, but it was easier work than writing for money.

"I need a real job," I finally admitted to Julie at brunch one morning, Isaac and Mingus' leashes entangled under our café table.

"There's an opening on the web team," Julie said.

"What? At your company?"

"Where else?"

"I don't know enough programming to work for a big corporation or anything, I was thinking more like... well, I don't know."

"First of all, it's not so much programming as project management. You're organized and you know how to write, so you can do that. And secondly, believe me, you know way more about web design than the guy who's leaving. He's a computer science guy — can't communicate with actual humans and everything he touches turns ugly."

"Is that why he's leaving?"

"No way. He's starting his own dot com."

Julie dragged me in for an interview with the interim head of marketing. It went well I guess, considering the fact that aside from academic essay writing all my work experience was in manual labour. "We'll call that technical aptitude, and excellent organizational skills," Julie had said when helping me finesse my CV.

"Don't forget to mention my love of alphabetical order," I

added, "and my extensive knowledge of the art and architecture of the second-century AD."

Julie sat in on the interview. I showed the interim head of marketing the freelance web design work I'd done.

"Quite creative," she said sceptically. "Why would you want to work in a corporate web-development environment like this?"

Good question. I gathered "for the money" would be the wrong answer.

"I like building things," I said. "I like fixing things, and I like putting things in order." All of these statements were true, but more so of Theo than of me.

"You could write fiction," Julie joked in the washroom after the interview.

"Do you think she bought it?" I asked, not at all sure I wanted the job.

"You'll get it," Julie said, and showed me around the building. The open office concept freaked me out. In this ocean of work, the desks formed rows like waves. "This is my desk," Julie said, "and the web team is over here." I'd get to sit next to her. That was the clincher.

I showed up for my first day of work wearing a cardigan, clutching a brown-bag lunch and a picture of my dog for my desk, still not convinced I wanted to work for a corporate web-development team. The job was nothing like I thought it would be. Julie had been right. Programming was the least of all the skills required. Diplomacy was far more important, and compromise, and patience. Oh, boy.

The first night I came home from work to Isaac's face in the front window, he was all waggle-butt happy to see me. The next morning there were some theatrics as I applied mascara and made for the door. "I'll be right back," I said, but he didn't buy it. The second night I came home to find one of my boots next to his basket. He hadn't chewed it, but he had cuddled with it, which, under the circumstances, seemed much worse.

"He has abandonment issues," I fretted to Theo. He thought Isaac would get over it, but I had my doubts. The whole time Isaac had lived with us I'd been home with him. Now, look what a traitor I'd turned out to be. By the end of my first week of my first-ever nine-to-five job I had depleted my supply of respectable outfits. I was sleep-deprived and deeply grouchy and Isaac was barely speaking to me.

"We've got to call in reinforcements," I said.

Over the next few weeks we asked everyone we knew, "Hey, want to borrow a dog?" Well, everyone except for Adrian. He was a big fan of Isaac, in theory.

"Look at that profile," he crooned to Isaac. "You two kind of look alike," he said of Isaac and me.

"Could we be in a John Singer Sergeant painting together?"

"Well, maybe in one of those Fido cellphone ads."

Finally, one morning, against Theo's better judgement, I dropped Isaac off at Adrian's on my way to work. I worried all day that by the time I picked him up that evening Adrian would have concocted a costume for him. Dog as bullfighter, or World War Two solider, one of those dressed-up-dog photographs you find in doctor's offices.

Adrian resented the insinuation. "He was born wearing a tuxedo, why mess with that?" Unfortunately, Adrian was so decadent-that it brought out the worst in the dog. After a few outings with him, Isaac was back to pulling on the leash like a lunatic. We took Isaac over to hang out with Mingus one morning. Julie and I took the bus home together, headed over to her place and found: one potted tree toppled, one bag of kibble looted, one laundry basket up-ended. Someone had nested in Julie's unmentionables.

"You dirty dog," I snapped Isaac's collar on him and dragged him home.

Theo and Isaac came home from the park one late-August day with the news that Wallace and Dee were back in town. The first thing I said was, "Maybe Isaac can go visit Box during the day." I was like a dog with a bone with this dog-sitter idea.

"I don't know," Theo said. "I gather they had a rough summer."

"On the Grand Manan? What could possibly go wrong there?"

We quickly fell into the same dog park routine with them. Dee was tight-lipped on the subject of their disastrous summer. Slowly we dragged the story out of Wallace. "His version, anyway," Theo kept reminding me.

A pparently, this past summer the family in the next cottage over from Wallace and Dee's had three kids and a Blue Heeler. Dee fell in love with that dog. She fell hard. And the feeling was mutual. The Blue Heeler followed Dee everywhere. They took long walks on the beach, often at mealtimes.

"All that stuff we got at the farmers' markets is going to waste," Wallace had hinted after a few hungry days.

"I'm on vacation," Dee said, and handed him a can opener.

"How about we go on a picnic tomorrow," Wallace suggested.

"How about you take a hike tomorrow," Dee smiled brightly.

Relations with the Blue Heeler's family soon became awkward. One night, Wallace and Box sat on the front step of their cottage listening to the Blue Heeler's family calling and calling for their dog, thinking that they'd lost him in the Fundy fog. Dee came home well past dark, tracking in sand and silver Blue Heeler hair, her pant legs still wet from the tide.

"I think you'd better lay off that dog for a while," Wallace said to his wife. Box sniffed her calves carefully, implying pretty much the same thing.

"That dog has a family," Wallace said. Dee ignored him. She reached under Box's front legs to pick him up, but Box wasn't having it. He got his back up in a hurry, hind legs splayed.

"Stubborn dog!" Dee dropped Box. His front paws landed heavily, like a prop-plane's wheels touching down. "Ungrateful…" she stormed off. There was only so far she could go in the cottage. First to the bathroom, then the bedroom. The groan of the rented mattress spoke volumes.

"Has to have everything his way…" Wallace heard her mutter through the flypaper-thin wall.

"Don't worry, she means me," he whispered into Box's velvet ear.

The Blue Heeler's family left the island the week after. And then a young American couple moved in — no kids, no dog. Wallace and Dee patched things up, for the sake of the summer. Dee took to cooking again and Wallace got pretty good with the hibachi. He made sure he washed every stray dish and Dee made sure Box got his fair share of long walks and five-dollar bones from the camp store.

"Let's go somewhere different next summer," Dee started in on Wallace on the queasy ferry ride home.

"But where?" Wallace squinted toward the mainland. He didn't think he had to have everything his way. But he did like for things to stay the same. He and Dee both knew the Grand Manan would never be the same after the Blue Heeler year.

Dee started researching new summer destinationss. Fall tourist info packets came in the mail. Wallace complained to us that she read sections out loud to him over dinner and left brochures on the back of the toilet, dog-eared pages for him to peruse.

By Christmas she had her heart set on the coast of Maine for next summer.

"The exchange rate is terrible though," Wallace confided to us one crisp evening. The dogs ran wild in the snow park. Box half disappeared in the fresh-fallen snow, deep as his legs were long. Isaac dove into drift after drift chasing his orange ball.

"Good thing he's black or we'd lose him," Theo said as we walked home single-file through sidewalk snow trails jaundice-yellowed by streetlamp light, Isaac panteding behind us.

"His tongue's a long story," I said. Wet footprints followed us inside.

Having a dog is less fun in winter. For the first time since moving to Montreal I invested in proper outerwear. A toque. A wind-proof jacket and snow-proof boots. It wasn't hard to see why Dee was so fixated on summer. She wrote away for information on Prince Edward Island. Wallace kept his mouth shut. Box's legs twitched in his sleep, running dreams that Wallace felt sure were of the Grand Manan. By Valentine's Day, Dee was an expert on the Gaspésie.

"But what do *you* think?" she prodded Wallace.

The only thing he could think to say was: "Our French isn't all that great."

"Well, I understand plenty," Dee said in a huff.

The next thing Wallace knew, Dee just wanted to stay home.

"Summer in the city?" Wallace and Box were sceptical.

"We've lived here fifteen years and never once taken in the Jazz Fest!" Dee insisted.

"Since when do you like Jazz?"

"Or the Fringe Fest, or the Film Fest… Montreal is the city of festivals."

"The City of Fest."

Dee brought home the schedules for every single festival, read advance reviews in the paper and made reservations for all the big shows. Every time we saw her she regaled us with the bio of some obscure musician she was suddenly a huge fan of, or gave away the plot of some play she couldn't wait to see.

"How come we never go to any of these festivals?" Theo asked.

"What are you asking me for? You're the one who's from here."

"Well, then, maybe I should look into getting us some tickets."

"Oh, please, don't start!" I said. Dee was driving me crazy with her "tickets for this" and "tickets for that." To be fair to Dee, pretty much everyone was driving me crazy. My job was starting to get to me. There were perks, of course. The health care plan, for one. It covered Theo too, because we were considered common-law married by now.

"Do you ever think about us getting married for real?" Theo asked me one evening, handing over a dental insurance claim.

"Don't let all that free dental work go to your head," I said.

"It's already gone to yours," he said. I was sporting some obscenely expensive new glasses, paid for by the company. All that late-night reading by flashlight had teamed up with the hundreds of hours a day I now spent in front of the computer to make me half blind. I didn't mind so long as someone else paid for it. We were taking our revenge on my job one insurance claim at a time, an eye for an eye and a tooth for a tooth.

"If we got married your father would come to the wedding, wouldn't he?"

"Good point. Divorce lawyers are always bad luck at weddings."

"Besides, I think it's best if your mother and my mother never meet."

One of the downsides to working for a multi-national corporation was the amount of travel involved. Sure it sounds glamorous, but the dog was less than impressed by my comings and goings. Telephone calls to and from Theo were constantly being cut off by elevators and airplanes. Sometimes everything would look familiar but then I'd be suddenly unsure about which city I was in. Sometimes I thought I'd stayed in this hotel before but I hadn't. Wherever I was, I woke up early enough to walk the dog. And then I missed him, because he wasn't there. Even when I was at home I kept a carry-on-sized suitcase half packed. If there was one thing Isaac truly hated, it was a suitcase.

If there was one person Isaac really loved, besides us, it was an old friend of Theo's whose real name I never knew. Theo always called her V. V wore very high heels and super skinny jeans. She had an impressive collection of fitted designer jackets that I studied carefully. "I've got to figure out where to get one of those," I told Theo. He laughed. He said V used to be a tomboy back in CEGEP and now she was making up for lost time. In the city, as far as I can figure, tomboys are girls who hang out with guys and watch hockey on TV. Where I came from the only difference between a tomboy and a regular girl is that a tomboy has shorter hair.

V wasn't the most dog-savvy person we'd ever met, but Isaac trusted her and we trusted him implicitly. She was so convinced that Isaac was a cartoon character that she gave him a nickname: Isaac the Wonder Dog. Isaac the Wonder Dog and Auntie V had many adventures together. It was hard not to laugh when I'd get a text message from V, in the middle of a meeting, written from

Isaac the Wonder Dog's point of view: *found a girls wallet in snow. v called her 4 me. im a hero!*

F riday afternoon, 5:40 Eastern Standard Time. Almost time to take the dog out and I was still at work, stuck in a conference call, tied to my desk with a phone wedged between my shoulder and my ear. Everyone else on the call was in California. Pacific Time. It was still the middle of the afternoon for them. They were all running full tilt on the premise that they would accomplish Many Other Things today. People kept joining the call and then leaving again. I couldn't keep track of who was on the line. We should have had this call last week but people had kept cancelling. Each time it got put off, I came to dread it more. Now it was finally unfolding — sloppy and mistrustful — just as I had feared.

It was the end of the day for me. The end of the week. I'd been at work for three more hours than anyone else on the call. I was wilted and done for. My dog was at home waiting, pacing, cocking his head and triangulating his ears to every little sound, none of which were me trucking up the stairs to unlock the front door. And worst of all, I had an echo on my line. We'd all experienced this kind of conference call echo before. Sometimes everyone can hear it; this time it was just me. I sounded like I was two inches tall and stuck in a tin can. Hearing my own voice distorted in this way made me feel edgy and inadequate: no matter what I said I felt as though my words lost weight and came out sounding hollow. I tried hanging up and calling back in but it didn't help. It was a continental issue — nothing to be done.

Don't even ask me what this meeting was about. Really, don't get me started. Every day was like one big, giant meeting interrupted only by the occasional change of scenery or the introduction of new characters. It was hard to get anything done with so many people panicking about how much stuff they had to get done. People were actually calling meetings to discuss previous and impending meetings.

Hank and I had had our own phone meeting before we went into this conference call. He was calling in from San Francisco, but we both worked on the same Web Team. I no longer thought it odd that a former farm girl like me, with an undergraduate degree in Art History, had wound up on the Web Team. Hank had a Master's degree in English Literature from UCSC. Our sys admin had gone through university on a football scholarship. He would have made it to the NFL too, were it not for a torn rotator cuff in his last semester. He was still in awesome shape. Which came in handy when we needed something from the director of IT, who was also huge, but all flab. He had studied computer science, but our running-back sys admin had figured it out on his own, which gave him a slight edge. My job on the Web Team was to do all the talking. It was a good thing the web came along when it did. What else would we, the unemployable, do for a living?

Hank and I had already agreed that we wouldn't be able to build the brand-new, online, event registration system that Marketing had been asking us for, even if we wanted to, which we didn't. We figured we had a perfectly acceptable contingency plan, but no. Liz, from Product Marketing, still wanted the whole shebang and would not be thwarted by technicalities. She said she didn't want to know about the "backend." She said it was too late for a "work-around."

"Honestly," I had complained to Theo while standing in the alley with Isaac after work one day, "our dog has better grammar than half the people I work with."

"It can't be worse than the way people mangle English in Montreal."

"Today I heard the word *architected* used in a sentence."

"Okay, that's bad," he agreed.

"Look, our dog just architected some poop."

L iz was at least six feet tall but she had a thing for small dogs. In the San Francisco office they were allowed to bring their dogs to work. There was a part-Schnauzer, part-Poodle kanoodling with a stuffed toy under Liz's desk, the kind of dog Isaac detested, the kind that never stopped barking. Liz claimed her dog knew 210 unique words. Apparently "contingency plan" were not among them.

Anthony was calling in from his cellphone on a highway between Venice Beach and Santa Monica. He worked with Julie on the Tradeshow Team. She said he was a great guy, but not so great to work with. Well, what's the point then? He started going on about a new online event registration system too. He was furious that no one had told him about any of this earlier, even though we had been trying to arrange this meeting for weeks. The buck-passing was escalating. Micro-management was emerging as a form of denial. Things were decidedly out of control. As the issues overlapped and became exaggerated people started taking things personally.

"This is *not* personal," I insisted to a woman named Sylvia. Our company had headhunted her from one of our largest competitors. She'd moved to San Francisco from Austin eight months ago, but hadn't quite arrived yet. We'd spoken on the phone often but never actually met. Hank had met her once. He said she was allergic to dogs, cats, dust and trees and had been not quite quietly advocating for a ban on the bring-your-dog to work policy. Good luck. The VP of Product Marketing had two Jack Russells and the VP of Industry Marketing had an Airedale. It would probably have been easier for Sylvia to leave California altogether.

I didn't know how I got off on the wrong foot with this woman from all the way across the continent, but at that moment I was not doing a very good job of reassuring her that we could make our existing event registration system work and this was making everyone else on the call anxious. I wished everybody would just calm down. THAT'S ENOUGH. Now GO LIE DOWN. I was so distracted by the echo on the line that I lost track of what I was saying. I was getting ahead of myself as I spoke. I was getting into trouble.

"All I'm saying is that we *already have* an online registration form for this type of event. We don't *need* to build an new one."

"Yeah," Hank piped up. "We can't keep re-inventing the wheel."

"Look, if you guys think I'm doing such a crap job here…" Sylvia was up a tree again, a tree that she was no doubt allergic to. Thanks a lot, Hank. He was right, of course, but I wished he wouldn't say it quite like that, because then Sylvia was telling us all over again how hard she'd been working. True, but the same could be said for everyone else, too. Then, sure enough, Liz was talking about how little bandwidth any of us had, which drove me crazy. Technically speaking, we had lots of bandwidth. We had a dual T3 for crying out loud, but I doubted anyone would appreciate that kind of humour at that point, so I kept my mouth shut.

No one wanted to hear why something didn't work; they just wanted you to make it happen for them. Some demands may very well have been technically possible, but that didn't make them a good idea. The more I tried to come up with a solution that worked for everyone, the more complicated everything seemed. The more I tried to simplify, the more muddled I felt. The empty sound of my voice on the phone line taunted me. To hell with technology, I thought. The phone doesn't even work.

Hank kept agreeing with everything I said, which, for some reason, made things worse. An echo in triplicate. I took off my glasses and put them on my desk. I was trying to convince Liz that even if the Web Team had the time to build a whole new system, it wouldn't work exactly the way Sylvia wanted it to. Anthony started talking about a completely different issue; I put my head in my hands. Who called this meeting, anyway? It was hard enough to reconcile the continent between us. The interdepartmental conflicts of interest were getting out of hand. I wanted to shout: STAY! But the phone would just twist my words.

Basically, as an employee of a multi-national corporation, I typed and talked on the phone for a living. When I got to the office in the morning, there were endless messages from San Francisco from the night before. When they got to work, they would have endless responses from Chicago, Montreal and New York. I knew not to expect responses from emails I sent off to Tokyo until the next day but I might catch Paris or Rome on the phone if I got to work early enough. The hours in which we all overlapped were so few. The time difference between Montreal and Paris was actually two weeks.

Staring out the window, I followed the movement of one very white cloud as it passed in front of a much darker cloud. Our ill-fated conference call bumbled on. Liz was now tearing into Hank. He'd gone spineless as a chew toy, intermittently emitting squeaks of protest. Sylvia seemed to be talking to someone else in the background. Somewhere someone's cellphone kept ringing and ringing.

Suddenly I felt a pair of hands, calm and cool on my shoulders. They rested there for a brief moment, and then I felt a light kiss on the side of my head, just above my telephone ear. I reached up behind me. My hand found her hair briefly, and then she was gone.

Julie. Her desk was three feet away from mine. Every day we bobbed and floated on the same tides of work, gossip, frustration and change. We heard each other's phone calls. We stole each other's blank CDs, file folders and envelopes. We helped each other with the little things — filling out expense reports, recovering disc space and booking hotels. We were on the same coast. We spoke the same language. Email washed over us in tides and wore us down until we were weary from it.

Sometimes we found time to eat lunch outside together, her floral skirts settling like sudden makeshift gardens in the patch of grass outside our office window. We never had the time during tradeshow season. The tradeshows were upon us again, like monsoons, but Julie's light touch was enough to interrupt my clouded thoughts.

Our call was still dragging on. Mercifully, I had stopped talking. I could see the situation clearly now, where I couldn't before. I envisioned the terrain of our call: we were all messing around in the waves, general splashing about having given way to fear, a loss of footing, flailing and shoving, yet grabbing for support. Sylvia, as it turned out, was ever so slightly afraid of the water. I was not the strongest swimmer either. I struggled to make my way toward her, to try and coax her to come ashore with me. Afraid I'd drag her down somehow, she panicked, kicked; her foot got me just below the knee. I lost my footing, sank slightly, and suddenly, I felt the undertow. The current carried me as far as it had to go and then unceremoniously released me. Shake. I shook my head like a wet dog and a salty pinwheel of water whirled from my hair, a spectacle captured briefly by the sun.

Instantly I was back at my desk. I raised the height of my swivel chair. I put my glasses back on. I reminded myself — I am three hours ahead. I speak from the future. I must go back in time to help get this call on track. Everyone was talking at once and no one was listening to each other.

"Sylvia," I interrupted. "Sylvia, I am going to be in San Francisco next week. Can we take this discussion 'offline' until then?"

She responded to Hank instead: "You know, I don't even know what you guys do, I mean besides post stuff on the web." I bit my tongue.

"Sylvia, what about Tuesday afternoon, what are you doing Tuesday afternoon? Can we meet?"

She blocked that attempt too: "I'm working like a dog non-stop all day on Tuesday," she replied. I sighed. I mean, how hard do most urban dogs work anyway? When we got home from a walk, Isaac went right back to his futon for yet more nap.

"Sylvia." My voice was calm. I was the only one who heard the echo when it bounced back at me as the other voices fell suddenly silent. "Sylvia, I would really like to get some face-time while I'm in San Francisco. Even if it's only for half an hour. I think it will make communication easier for us going forward." I couldn't believe I had to resort to such corporate-speak. Sylvia sighed audibly, unaware of how much she was telling me with that sigh — she was going to make a date with me to get me off her back and then blow me off at the last minute. I didn't care anymore. I'd deal with that eventuality if and when the time came.

"So, Wednesday, say three or four in the afternoon, can you make some time?"

"Okay, which do you want, three or four?"

She was still suspicious. Like a pound puppy, scared of its own shadow. What had they done to her at that other company, before she came to us? I felt so helpless against the tide of the call that I clung to this idea of a face-to-face meeting like a dog's jaws clamped down on his new favourite stick in a back alley tug-of-war.

"Let's say four," I told her, "and I'll confirm with you when I look at my flight information."

Liz was suddenly cheerful. "So, we can all be friends now?"

It was hard to say if we were even slightly further along than we were before this meeting, but Liz took this agreement between Sylvia and I as some kind of point of closure. The West Coast rushed off to the rest of their day.

I hung up the phone with grim satisfaction at 7:15 PM Friday evening. I hoped Theo was home by now. Otherwise, the dog would be pissed. Or not, as the case may be. The phone rang again almost immediately. I cringed, but the call display told me it was just Julie calling from downstairs, offering me a ride home. I gratefully accepted. I reminded myself that my workday was now over. I forced myself to resist the temptation to read any of the thirty-seven emails that had found their way to me during the time of the call. There would be more before the West Coast day was done.

While my computer was shutting down for the weekend, I stood up, raised my arms straight up in the air and twisted my torso side to side. The waters seemed calmer now. We'd weathered yet another storm. Julie was waiting downstairs. Maybe we'd get together this weekend for a walk with the dogs. After trying so hard to keep my tongue in check all week, I spoke whatever came to my mind just to hear my own thoughts again. Now that my call was over my voice came out clear and definitive, "LET'S GO HOME."

There was only so much of that job I could take before I started to concoct escape plans. Long lunches, personal phone calls on the company dime. Carving a few hours out of a business trip to try to see something more than conference rooms and hotel bars. I made Theo read *The Phantom Tollbooth;* I felt so much like Milo again. Always wishing I were somewhere else. When I was at work I couldn't wait to get home. At home all I could talk about was work. I'd stand in the kitchen cooking dinner with a vengeance.

"I hate my job," I'd rant, waving a kitchen knife for punctuation.

"Even the dog hates your job," Theo pointed out.

One day, Isaac the Wonder Dog decided he wanted to go visit his Auntie V over in Outremont. He asked us and we asked Auntie V and she said: "Oui! Isaac the WD (IWD) can visit me. Heck, he can stay all week." This was excellent timing as we, Isaac the WD's mom and dad (m+d), also known as the Isaac the Wonder Dog Support Staff, were much in need of a vacation.

In advance of these concurrent vacations, Auntie V issued a press release stating that she intended to spoil the Wonder Dog rotten. We assured Auntie V that hanging out with a dog for the afternoon was one thing, but having a dog spend the week with you was quite another. In addition to providing Auntie V with a nine-page manual on How to Own and Operate This Dog, detailing the WD's top seven emergency phone numbers, his food and walking schedule, tips on how best to play ball both inside the house and out, as well as disciplinary guidelines and various strategies for keeping one step ahead of the dog, we the Isaac the Wonder Dog Support Staff also issued this list of Words the Dog Knows in a pre-emptive effort to preserve Auntie V's sanity.

It should be noted that Isaac the Wonder Dog knows more words than these, but we did not wish Auntie V to think we were either bragging or crazy. For the purposes of this document, *you* refers to Auntie V:

ISAAC — The dog knows his name because it's the word he hears most often. That said, he also responds to: Peaches, Pookie, Pumpkin, Sweet Pea, Noodle, Poodle, Buddy and Handsome, as in, "Hello, Handsome." Basically, he knows when you're talking to him. And he loves it. Feel free to make up your own pet names.

NO — No is the most important word in the dog's vocabulary. Don't be afraid to use it.

SIT — If at first he doesn't sit, repeat until he sits. Pointing at the ground helps.

GO LIE DOWN — This should not be used as a punishment. It's more of a suggestion. Sometimes he thinks it's his duty to stick around and entertain you. Sometimes he just doesn't know how tired he is. In either case, once he's told to do so he's very happy to go take a nap.

GO LAY DOWN — Same as above, plus he's flexible about bad grammar.

UP — This can apply to anything. Especially useful for couches and stairs. Or if he's lying on something and you want him to get off it. Or if he's just lying there staring at you because he doesn't believe it's really finally honest and for true time to go out.

DOWN — Like up, down can also apply to anything, but used less often. He's not a jumper, our dog.

STAY — Use at intersections, in the alley to get him to wait while you get the leash off him, and in the house when you're leaving a room but coming right back, because sometimes he'll follow you from room to room. Once again, pointing helps get the message across.

OKAY — For when the staying is done, or, for example, when it's safe to cross the street.

IT'S OKAY — For when he's afraid of something, like lightning, of which he is very afraid. Or for when he thinks you're mad at him, especially if you were mad at him but now you're over it. You will know he's afraid of something if he comes over and leans on your leg and/or tries to crawl under your desk. You will know he thinks you're mad at him if he starts staring at you with a hangdog look.

NO SNORFFELLING — For when you're grating parmesan, or any kind of cheese, and he's suddenly standing very close to you, looking up at you in a way that begs you to defy all "no people food" rules, or, just after you've grated cheese, and he's nose to the ground all over the kitchen floor like some kind of Third-World-beggar-urchin dog.

YOU WANT TO GO OUT? YOU WANT TO GO FOR A WALK? READY? — Ask him in just the right way, and he'll stick his ears out and cock his head at you in an irresistible manner commonly known as triangle ears. It's tempting to ask him if he's ready, just to see what it does to his ears. But please, don't ask if you don't mean it.

WHERE'S YOUR BALL? — Useful for getting ready to leave the house. He'll go find his ball and bring it to you so you don't have to hunt high and low.

NOT THAT BALL. WHERE'S YOUR OTHER BALL? — Useful if he brings you a tennis ball when what you want is an orange ball, or if he brings you a busted ball when in fact there is a much better ball floating around your apartment somewhere. As you will soon discover, all balls fall into a ball hierarchy that cannot be messed with.

DROP — An indispensable word in ball play. If you throw the ball he will bring it back to you, but he will not always put it down so you can throw it again. If you try and pull a ball or a stick from his mouth he thinks you're playing the pulling game. He always wins the pulling game.

OVER HERE — For when he wants to play ball in the kitchen while you're doing dishes or cooking, but he's put the ball way too far away from you for you to kick it. Or for when you're in the alley and you want him to run around behind you so you don't kick the ball directly into him.

COME — He loves this one. Except when it's late at night and he's sniffing in slow motion, stopping to examine every fencepost and pee-soaked patch of grass.

LET'S GO — For when you've really had it with the slow-motion sniffing on the late walk.

THAT'S ENOUGH — You have to tell him sometimes, because he really doesn't know.

The following is a third-hand account of the adventures Isaac the Wonder Dog had during his week with Auntie V. Much of this narrative was compiled from the WD's own notes. We filled in the rest. Purely for comparison purposes, we provide you here with a before portrait of Auntie V and Isaac the Wonder Dog:

First night: m+d say we're just going for an extra-long walk, but they don't fool me. We're headed straight for Auntie V's place and they're lugging all my gear. Auntie V's stairs are very steep. I stand out on her balcony and watch m+d disappear down the street. Auntie V lets me sleep in her bedroom, even though I snore. The next morning m+d take the train to Toronto. On the train there're babies in front of them, babies beside them, screaming babies behind. Birth control for the rest of the year! Disgusted by this public display of excessive procreation, m+d refrain from calling Auntie V to worry over me.

Second night: V says m+d are having no fun without me. I send them a text message, with Auntie V's assistance. *auntie v ruined her sandals playin ball w me in the alley — shes so cool. 8 my dinner, now im napping.*

Third night: I text m+d again, so they don't forget about me: *went w auntie v 2 visit M, taught him to play ball.* (Note that M is a boy, approximately seven years old.)

Fourth night: I almost drop dead from heat. Auntie V almost drops dead from heat too. But as far as m+d know, everything is fine. They leave Toronto for points westward, where they will spend two nights with a friend in the countryside. Auntie V was informed of this plan, I was not. As far as I know m+d are never coming back.

Fifth night: 10:14 PM m+d get a text message from Auntie V that reads: *guess who just got skunked. fuck. fuckin fuck fuck. fk.* A flurry of text messaging ensues. I get a tomato juice bath but I still stink. Auntie V gets stinking drunk and at 4 AM she punches her friend Dan. She thinks. In the morning she can't remember. It will take weeks to sort that one out.

Sixth night: Auntie V texts m+d: *has pooch had rabies shot? got it in the mouth — still buggin him a bit. tomato juice better not fucking count as people food.*
    m+d had sternly warned Auntie V against feeding me people food, but she went ahead and washed my mouth out with tomato juice anyway. And it did the trick!
    m+d text: *u r our hero.*

Seventh night: Things are calming down around here. m+d have yet to return.
    m+d text: *has skunk stench abated? r u + Isaac still friends?*
    Auntie V: *we r much better. back 2 scaring hassidic kids in the alley.*
    m+d: *u 2 r bonded 4 life now!*
    Auntie V: *4 life 2 long. till wed ok.*

On Wednesday m+d were reunited with Isaac the Wonder Dog. By then Auntie V's apartment didn't smell like skunk at all, though m+d had tacitly agreed that even if it did they would swear it didn't. Auntie V reminded us that she had warned us before we left that there were skunks in her 'hood. And we didn't take her seriously at all. As the after portrait clearly indicates, Isaac and Auntie V came out of the skunk stench scandal smelling like roses and, yes, they remained friends.

After spending the week with Isaac the Wonder Dog Auntie V issued this statement:

> *Sure, Isaac knows his name and a ton of ball-chasing and walking commands. Big deal. m+d don't give Isaac enough credit for the theoretical aspect of his vocabulary, which I was fortunate enough to coax out of him when I wasn't scaring him by screaming at the TV. Here then, is an updated list of some of the words Isaac the Rhetorical Wonder Dog knows. (Sadly, he still has problems with his citation skills). Thanks Isaac, for all your help with my dissertation this past week. xo, Auntie V.*

HEGEMONY — At first there was the reign of m+d. Now, whatever Auntie V says, goes.

HOME — Home is where they keep the kibble. Home is both the origin and the terminus of the walk. Locus of the soundest sleeps, at home all scents are known.

CYBERSPACE — The place were people go while dogs are sleeping.

INFINITY — In the time between sleep and waking there is the great nothingness of the nap.

CONQUEST — The ball is a living thing. It is not enough to give chase, catch the ball in mid-air and bring it back for another throw. A victory lap is in order. And then give it a good shake to make sure that it knows it has been conquered.

CONTINGENCY — If an orange ball has just been lost, under a fence, say — look around. Maybe there's a busted tennis ball nearby. Maybe there's a stick just waiting to be found.

PHENOMENOLOGY — When wind happens it happens in the ears. When rain happens all the smells are hidden. When thunder happens it happens inside the heart and head and there is no hiding from the fear.

CONSUMPTION — If it is put in front of you, eat it. If it is on the floor, eat it. If it is on the ground, eat it. If it is dead, sniff it carefully, and then eat it. Even if it smells like shit, eat it. Even if it is shit, eat that too.

CORRUPTION — One way to make a walk last longer is to walk slower. Stop everywhere, sniff everything and then run a little as if to catch up, as if you're not up to anything at all. But don't push it, or they'll put you on the leash.

SECURITY — The leash makes pedestrians feel more secure. Barking keeps the balcony free from cats. Bark if the doorbell rings. Everyone knows evil smells feline, and danger rings before it enters.

TRUST — When they say: "We'll be right back," they may not come *right* back, but they always do come back eventually. When they say: "It's all right," it may not be all right yet, but it will be soon. When they say: "Stay," for no apparent reason, it's best to just do it. Who knows, maybe there's a car coming.

PHANTASMAGORIA — Dog-shaped blurs dot the distant horizon, man-shaped shadows move through the night time, footsteps fall down from the ceiling, disembodied voices float up through the floorboards, ghost scents waft on the wind.

WORK — Play is a re-enactment of work. The ball is a bird, see? Shake it, make sure it's dead. These sticks need rounding up. Who left this branch here? The work dog is ill suited to tagging along to the laundromat and no good at all at pacing the video store aisles — all the movies smell the same.

PERFORMANCE — If you bring them the ball they will throw it. If you stare at the door they will open it. If you come when you are called, you will usually get something out of it. If you lose a ball under the couch they will find it for you. People are easy to train.

TRANSFIGURATION — When the woman puts mascara on it means she's leaving the house. When the man puts big boots on it means the alley has been erased by snow. When the black cat has a white stripe on it's back, be careful! The world can change in an instant.

MELANCHOLIA — When playtime is over and the long nap in the dark is over, and the early morning walk is over, sometimes in a hurry, sometimes even in the rain, the people shut the door behind them and the dog is left to his lonesome.

If you hate your job it's best not to go on vacation. The longer you're away the harder it is to go back again. After our week in Toronto, I wanted at least another week off at home.

"No one's forcing you to stay at this job," Theo reminded me for the umpteenth time. Julie had said as much to me as well. It was true. I'd made my last student loan payment months ago. I had more than enough money saved to do something... if only I could figure out what. I kept having this restless dream that it was winter and I had never left the farm. My father had ordered me out into the beginnings of a snowstorm to bring the cattle down from the northwest pasture to the barn. Red's hooves struck the iron-cold earth in a skittish canter, made irregular by the force of the wind. Dry pockets of snow began to accumulate in the frozen tufts of brown grass. The cattle grudgingly consented to be herded toward shelter. As we progressed, my dream shifted. The path before us straightened, fitted stones appeared to pave the way. The snow and the cold melted into warmth and colour along the Via Appia.

Onward, toward the cattle markets of the Foro Boarium we drove, past mausoleums, catacombs and all nature of crumbling ruins.

I worried that this dream would lead to another trip back to Nova Scotia. Theo seemed to think the dream would lead to Rome. My company had an office in a highrise in a modern suburb of Rome. I'd been there once, for an all-day meeting with the director of Support and Services for Europe. I'd been to Paris and Amsterdam too, for meetings in conference rooms that could have been anywhere.

"We could drive down to Vermont next weekend," I said.

"How about you turn your cellphone off next weekend," Theo said. "That would be a vacation."

"That plan's so crazy it just might work."

The next weekend, Theo and I packed a picnic lunch and headed for the park with Isaac. The plan was to spend the afternoon *far away from business cares,* as Horace would say, lying on the grass, reading in the sun. The wind had other ideas.

"This wind is no picnic."

"This picnic isn't exactly a walk in the park."

While I was attempting to wrestle our picnic blanket to the ground, Isaac ran off after another dog. Theo chased after the two of them. They were gone for a worryingly long time. What if there'd been an accident? I should never have left my cellphone at home! I would have flagged down the next cellphone-wielding passer-by if Isaac had not come bounding back to the blanket just then, followed by the most mixed-up-looking mutt I'd ever seen.

"What the heck kind of dog are you?" I asked her. She flopped down to the ground and rolled on her back in the grass. Isaac stood panting and wagging, his tongue hanging out, half a foot long at least.

"Hey Simone!" Theo hollered and waved from across the park. He was walking with a smallish woman. The mutt's owner, I presumed.

"I'd like to introduce you to someone," he said as they approached.

"Professor Azar?" I couldn't believe it. She had her hair up in a ponytail; she was wearing jean shorts. Does not compute.

"Call me Vita," she said.

"You two know each other?" Theo and I asked each other, almost in unison.

"Remember that essay on the invention of the classical that I was working on that weekend we met?" I asked Theo. "That was for Professor Azar's class."

"Vita," she said again.

"The paper was late because of him," I told her. She laughed.

"Theo was a student of mine at UQAM," she said. News to me. He'd worked as her research assistant one summer too — years before I arrived in Montreal. I had no idea she'd taught at UQAM. I didn't even know she spoke French. The ten-year age difference between Theo and me remained full of surprises.

"So what have you been up to?" she asked me.

I started to tell her about my job, about the politics, the stress, and the travel, and once I got going I couldn't stop. "I have a hundred and seventy thousand Air Miles saved up, and no time to spend them because I'm travelling so much for work."

"I can't tell if you love it or hate it," Vita said.

"She loves to hate it," Theo said. "Tell her about the time you woke up in Rome."

"God it was awful. I didn't get to see anything! My boss and I flew in from Paris late at night, slept in a generic hotel, and then spent the whole day in a meeting in a highrise in EUR, you know that fascist-modernist suburb Mussolini built? What a surreal place. Anyway, it was dark out by the time we went to dinner. A taxi drove us, at breakneck speed, through these massive, ancient walls, and then we were in a traffic circle, racing round the Colosseum. STAY, I wanted to say… But then it was gone. Or we were…"

"Have you considered going back?" Vita asked me.

"What, and quit my job?"

"Well, I was thinking for a vacation… but yes, why not quit?"

"Sold!" Theo said, so quickly that immediately I suspected him of orchestrating this whole encounter with Vita in the park.

"What are you two up to?"

"Well," Vita shot Theo a quick glance. So they were in cahoots! "Some new sites have been opened by the *Soprintendenza Archeologica di Roma* that I need to document, but I don't have time to go myself. I can't pay you anything, but if you can book a flight with your Air Miles then I can offer you a place to stay for free. My uncle's wife's sister's apartment in Cipro is empty for one month."

Whoa. The wind blew a twig in my hair. I plucked it out. Isaac examined it to see if it counted as a stick or not. Decided it did not.

"But what about Isaac?" I said, stalling for time.

"Buddy and me will be fine," Theo said.

"This dog hates suitcases," I explained lamely to Vita. We all knew I was already packing my bags in my head.

When we travel by plane to a distant place, we travel through time as well as through space. We sleep, or do not, high over the Atlantic. We fly through the restless twisted night, hip-to-thigh with strangers. We breakfast over the Alps. Diamond lakes glint like lost earrings in long foothills of glacier-combed hair. When we land — disgruntled, dishevelled and delayed — we have only just ceased leaving. Arrival takes much longer still. Our baggage thunks onto the carousel. It inches toward us. It catches up with us. Outside, there are armed guards and palm trees and no one told us how hot it would be. We are new, we are strange, we are temporary. We should have known. We haven't travelled to a foreign place. We are foreign. Nothing is as we think it will be.

Vita's uncle's wife's sister's apartment was really only one room plus a kitchenette, in a working-class neighbourhood tucked in behind Vatican City. The place seemed even smaller with the windows open for all the street sounds to crowd in. I locked the massive green front door behind me and walked out into Rome.

In Rome at last it was plain to see how many of the slides Vita had shown us in class had been photographs taken by her. She had taught us her own perspective. Following in her footsteps, I stood where she had stood; I saw what she had once seen and photographed and shown to me, and countless other students. At every ruin I envisioned her lithe form passing in front of the slide projector's floating images of stone. The sunlit city refused to solidify. For the first few days I stayed lost in the dark, medieval quarters, where the frailer light would have drowned itself in the black shadows of her hair.

Fragments of photographs and portions of texts affixed themselves to my surroundings. No cattle clogged the Forum, as they did in paintings by Claude. Only tourists. The Circus Maximus was really just a grassy field. The Mausoleum of Augustus endured

an overgrown state similar to the ruins of the farmhouse in the northwest pasture of my parents' farm. Dilapidated stray cats of every size and description lounged in the relative safety afforded by cordoned-off historical sites. Stray dogs were a rare sight in the city, though occasionally one did see small packs trotting down side streets purposefully. A glimpse of these strays made me miss Isaac much more than the dogs on leashes did. He'd been a stray once, abandoned. Someone had thrown him to the wolves, as it were, and we'd saved him. I didn't dare go anywhere near the wild dogs of Rome for fear of rabies or worse. Apparently, all over Italy, people were leaving the countryside for the cities, and leaving their dogs behind. Packs of these domesticated dogs gone wild were decimating the native wolf population. Occasionally a pack would wander into an abandoned village, foraging for food. Toenails on medieval cobblestones the only sound in town.

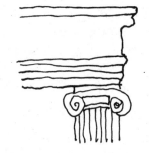

In Rome I dreamt of cattle again: I glimpsed them through the pillars of the Temple of Castor. They were being led to the Campo Vaccino, where they would be sold at auction. I could smell them from where I sat, on a ruined segment of a column on the floor of the Foro Romano. At first I was alone in the landscape of antiquity. The sun shone, warming me, warming even the indifferent stone. The cattles' hooves raised a din of dust; the humid heat of the day dissuaded the dust from spreading. Tails swatted flies away from pale hides, listlessly, in the middle distance. The brightness bore down on me. Soon the landscape began to fill in. Painters arrived and set up their easels. The scenery became hazy with brush stroke. The ruins shifted themselves for the sake of better composition. Aromas of linseed and turpentine wafted over the close smell of the cattle *en plein air.* An awful-sounding cloud arose, and grew menacing: as if one bumblebee, lacking in ambition, was suddenly drowned out by a swarm of wilful wasps fleeing their grey paper nest.

I awoke, convinced that I had been stung. There was no sun in the waking Rome, only the pale paper dome of early morning. The tourists had not all arrived yet, though many were on their way. There were no cattle, only the sound of wasps. Vespas swarming the main arteries; Via Angelo Emo on to Candia, around Vatican City, around Castel Sant'Angelo, they buzzed about the city's stone veins, vibrated in the narrow viccolos like breath through the whetted reed of a clarinet. My windows shook with all they had to say.

The pretext Vita had offered for my time in Rome was pretty flimsy. Her short list of archaeological sites could have been documented within a week anywhere else in the world. Factor in an extra week at least, given the Roman round-about bureaucracy. I had all month, and my own private tour guide to boot. Vita had arranged for me to meet with a Roman friend of hers.

"What kind of friend?"

"Barbara will help you make arrangements," was all she'd said. At first I assumed Barbara had been a former student of Vita's, but no. Barbara had studied Tourism, which, in Rome, is almost the same as studying Art History.

"Only to make more money is possible, yes?" Barbara joked. For a while I thought Vita was paying Barbara to take care of me, but Barbara denied this.

"It is a pleasure to me," she said.

Barbara was my only Roman friend. Like most Romans, she worked in the city and lived in the suburbs. On Saturdays she worked only in the morning. Saturday afternoons she entertained me — at least she had so far.

One Saturday we visited the Castelli Romani. I waited for Barbara at the Arco di Travertino metro stop, where she parked her car. Barbara drove slowly, a dangerous thing for a Roman driver to do. At first I clutched at the dashboard like an old woman every time we braved an intersection, until finally she told me, "Don't to worry. This is the only car that I have."

There was no choice but to trust Barbara: to not kill us, even when she was shout-talking in Roman dialect on her cellphone; to always know where we were going, even if not how to get there; and to always be late, unless I was late, in which case she would be early. Most days I was early and she was very late.

We headed south on Via Appia Nuova. I knew this because I had a map. Barbara swore that whenever Romans wanted directions they asked tourists, because all tourists had maps. Maybe, but my map did not in any way indicate the fine-toothed aqueducts that combed the clipped fields on either side of us.

"Look!" I pointed.

"Bah," Barbara said. "I see them every day."

I told Barbara I wanted to see Via Appia Antica, the part that still had sections of ancient Roman paving stones. But she said, "No, it's too bumpy to drive there."

Later that evening, on the way home from a late dinner outside of Frascati, Barbara informed me that we were driving on Via Appia Antica.

"Right now?" I asked. It was too dark for me to consult my map, and I was often confused about time in Rome. I had no past there yet, and Barbara's English had no past perfect.

"Yes," she said. "But not in this section of which you speak," referring to the ancient Roman paving stones, I supposed.

The road was narrow, high-walled and dark. We almost failed to see a stopped car ahead of us. Swerving to avoid it, we just missed the protruding ass of a prostitute leaning into the rolled-down window of the car. Barbara made a menacing hand gesture.

"You see — Roman drivers! They stop anywhere they like!"

The next week, when Barbara and I met at Arco di Travertino, we arrived at the same time. I took this rare instance of mutual punctuality as a good sign, but Barbara found it disturbing. "There must to be a reason," she insisted.

According to my map, we were driving out of Rome on Via Tuscolana. Barbara stopped the car suddenly to point out two ancient buildings. They were medieval, but Barbara used the word *ancient* whenever she meant *old*. She said an auto mechanic owned the buildings. He did very good work, but he couldn't expand his business. Because his buildings were considered historic, he was forbidden to make any changes to them. I couldn't tell whether Barbara thought this was funny, stupid, or sad.

Traffic rushed past us.

"Barbara. Last week you complained that Roman drivers stop their cars in the road, but now you stop in the road."

"I am a Roman. When I say the Romans do something, it is because I also do this thing."

We slipped back into the stream of traffic. Long umbrella pines lined the road. Humpbacked aqueducts chased us out of Rome.

…NVMENTIS, EX VESTIGIIS VIDELICET ÆDIFICIOR., MOENIVM
…LINISQ COLLECTA, VETER, DENIQ AVCTORVM FIDE CONFIRMAT,IN HĀC
…IN QVAS VRBEM DIVISIT IMP. CÆSAR AVGVSTVS.
…Roma adpellata, situ primo fuit quadrato, Tribus, uel ut Plinius, quatuor distincta portis vario ambitu cō
…XIIII. diuisa, sed ualles deinde, locaq, depssa, propter amplißimos fornices superaedificatos, iti mōtib. æquata
…ria perierint, prsens tamen tabella, ea ōia accurate exhibet, qua spectator beneuolus sumptu nō magno frui potest.

ORIENS

Villa Creperci ani

Aqua Antoniana

Via Gabina & Prænestina

Via Latina

Hippodromus Aureli

Amphitheatrum

Marciana Insula

PVTICVLI

Lavernium

REGIO

The Palatino Hill was once the most exclusive neighbour-hood in Rome, the Hollywood Hills of the ancient world, home to senators and emperors, forever tearing down and rebuilding, each villa more extravagant that the last. These rich and powerful ghosts still had enough cachet to attract some of the most pretentious tourists I'd encountered yet. I cringed as a man behind me hollered overly familiar, with a heavy Long Island accent, "Okay kids, let's go over to Livia's house." Only in mod-ern Rome did suburban American families visit the house of the wife of an emperor every day. My mother's bedtime stories about the Roman Empire and my father's rants about American Imperialism had finally merged into one big, badly-dressed, loud, over-priced, over-crowded nightmare.

The tourists complained openly about the Italians. Lazy, crooked, insolent, impossible, monkeys, they called them. I com-plained bitterly about the tourists to Barbara.

"Why you think you are better than them?" she asked me.

The next day I wrote a postcard to my parents: *Every day Rome is invaded by tourists. I have joined the barbarous hoards.*

It took Barbara two full weeks to convince park officials to let us into the Farnese Gardens. The site was closed to the pub-lic, but it was on Vita's list so I was determined to get in. I thought two weeks was slow, but no. Gradually, I gathered that in Rome any decision made in under a month's time was considered hasty. Finally, when permission was granted, it came by way of a letter on heavy paper bearing a hand-inked signature and an embossed crest.

Barbara and I made our way across the Domus Tiberiana. I was lugging a camera bag and heavy tripod through the mid-day sun and Barbara was telling me a story about how most Italians don't travel in Italy until they're old, "Because then it is very easy for them, very close, no?"

My cellphone rang. Six rings to find it in my camera bag. It was Theo. He rarely called me out of the blue.

"Isaac and I were just in the park," he said.

"And?" I asked impatiently. It was about ten in the morning in Montreal. I was just about to set the tripod up within a few feet of where Nero had allegedly stood, fiddling. This spot of the Palatino would indeed have offered an excellent view of Rome ablaze. Theo and I were talking across a time zone difference just shy of two thousand years.

"He was running with a pack of dogs and this other guy was throwing a ball for them."

"That's great," I said, recalculating. The time difference between us was actually considerably longer than two thousand years. Somewhere on this hill, rumour has it, Romulus and Remus were suckled by a she-wolf. Now hand-lettered signs read: *Pleased to Not Feed Cats*.

"Then the ball disappeared."

"So what? He loses balls all the time."

"Well, it was a small ball."

"Oh, my God." I put the tripod down.

"Yeah. The other guy and I, we were hunting all over for it and it just wasn't anywhere. I looked at Isaac and he had this look on his face."

"You think he swallowed it?"

"I know he did. I'll take him to the vet tomorrow."

If Theo believed it, then I believed it, but it hardly seemed real.

I tried to explain the situation to Barbara. We quickly ran into linguistic difficulties. The difference between eating a ball and swallowing one was, to me, a small but all-important distinction.

One that I could not make clear.

I showed Barbara a picture of Isaac, and told her how much I missed him. She said, "You cannot miss this dog." Meaning, I decided, you cannot forget him.

"What's the word for dog?" I asked.

"*Cane.*"

For the rest of my time in Rome, I confused the words *cane* and *carne* — remarking on the wild meats of Rome and asking at restaurants for food with no dog in it. Theo continued to text me with updates on the ball-in-dog situation. The vet took four different X-rays before admitting that it was possible that there was a ball in the dog.

"Possible, but improbable," he said.

"If you could have seen the look on Isaac's face," Theo told me on the phone.

"We can look for a new vet when I get home."

There were days in Rome when I didn't speak to anyone, when I couldn't speak, because I knew no Roman tongues, and all day long I was overwhelmed by fragments: headless statues littering the gardens, and museums full of shelves of heads of stone. For days on end I roamed alone, *Oxford Archaeological Guide* tucked under my arm, my camera bag in tow.

Even if I wanted to, I could not seek answers to ineffectual questions.

"How long will it take?"

"It is impossible to know this."

What I wanted I could not say.

Saturday afternoons, Barbara and I stumbled over ancient, elegant things. Our conversations tumbled through all possible combinations of *inglese, francese, fratalian* and *franglais.* My English slowed to a crawl, which was just as well, as there were no words for the inert and inarticulate stones we witnessed. Long, smooth shanks of broken columns, once supportive, now useless, but still so well preserved.

"Here, take it home with you," Barbara said, squatting to pretend-lift a Corinthian capital. She enjoyed this joke. "We have so many... We have so much of these things."

"Where do you go in Rome?" Her friends pooled their small handfuls of English to ask me, mystified by my interest in all things ancient. They were chasing after modern: the latest fashion, the best food, the most elusive men.

"Simone goes only in the underground of Rome," Barbara answered for me. I laughed, letting them believe this, though it was not technically true. The archaeological sites I frequented were indeed metres beneath the street level of the modern city. But I also had a thing for open-air fruit and vegetable markets. Campo dei Fiori was the obvious one. My favourite was the larger market on Via Andrea Doria, near my apartment in Cipro. Old women shopped there, stout housewives haggled there, with vendors who ignored them studiously, shouting instead, musical obscenities over the shoppers' heads, to the gods, to the other vendors and to the gypsy children who buzzed around the edges of everything, fast and hungry as flies.

One afternoon at the market on Andrea Doria, I stood in silent awe in front of a basket of fresh, handpicked, porcini mushrooms so fat and brown and expensive I could have cried. The vendor burbled at me — *prego, signorina* this and *prego, signorina* that — not encouraging me to buy but rather urging me to move aside as I was blocking the way for paying customers. As I turned reluctantly to leave, my ear tripped on the unmistakeable sound of someone speaking Québécois French. I followed the accent through the market until I found its source: two women deep in a heated discussion over whether or not punterella could be cooked the same way as broccoli rape. *"Non, c'est plus comme chicorée,"* I said excitedly, introducing myself as a *Montréalaise*. We fell into conversation with the immediacy of compatriots, switching back and forth between French and English just as we do *chez nous*. One of the women was from Quebec City. She'd been living in Rome for three months, at the Quebec Arts Council's Studio in Monteverde Vecchio. I was impressed. I didn't know Quebec had an Arts Council. Note to self. The other woman was visiting from Montreal. She'd be returning in two days. I had less than a week left in Rome.

"We should meet up when you get back," she said, and I agreed. She handed me her card. I stared at her street address in disbelief.

"I live on Saint-Urbain Street too," I said. "On the same block, I think."

"I'm in the place next to the giant rosebush," she said.

"We're just a few doors down from there," I said. "Our front door is purple…"

"How come I've never seen you?" she asked.

"Maybe you've seen my dog," I said. "He's black, with an orange ball."

"I see that dog everyday, but always with a man."

"That would be my boyfriend."

"Wow, and all this time I thought he was this lonely guy, just him and his dog."

"No," I assured her. "He has a lazy girlfriend waiting at home."

When I called Theo later to tell him this story. He said, "But you're never alone with a dog!"

Vita's uncle's wife's sister had rented out the apartment in Cipro to tourists for the summer, so I had to be out by the end of June. I left it to Barbara to decide what we'd do on my last afternoon.

"*Passagiatta*," she suggested on the phone.

"Fine," I said without bothering to ask what *passagiatta* was. It could have been a kind of pastry or a new shoe store for all I knew. Barbara's cellphone explanations were rarely elucidating.

"Meet me at Piazza Venezia, you will see."

The 496 bus was not running from Cipro so I arrived at Piazza Venezia very late for our date. Barbara had been early, for once. "You are late!" she said, pointing at her watch with mock ferocity and then laughing. "You are a real Roman now, yes? We must to give you the key of the city."

As we passed beneath Mussolini's balcony Barbara said, "*Caio Duce*," giving what I presumed to be an imitation of Il Duce's wave. The Corso was a crush. *Passagiatta* appeared to be a communal shuffle up the street. Sunday afternoon and half the city had turned out for no other purpose than to walk from bottom to top in a slow parade of see and be seen.

"They do this every Sunday?"

"Yes, and in the villages too."

The crowd carried us along. Impossible not to feel a part of it, embedded as we were, shoulder-to-shoulder, in perfume and body odour, in private jokes and cellphone conversations, jostles, jibes and loud flirtations.

The *passagiatta* spat us out of the Corso into the Piazza del Popolo. Barbara and I made our way through the crowd to the far side of the square, to sit in the afternoon sun on the steps of the Santa Maria del Popolo. The preamble to good-bye began. I invited Barbara to visit us in Montreal one more time, though this seemed like an increasingly futile gesture. Not because Barbara wasn't interested in Montreal — she was, or claimed to be. But she already had a long list of places she wanted to visit. And, being in the tourism business herself, she could only travel in the off-season. I couldn't in good conscience recommend Montreal in November to anyone.

"Yes, but is very beautiful there, no? Vita has told me," Barbara said lazily. We fell into a post-*passagiatta* stupor, rousing ourselves only to follow the sun's slow climb up the church steps.

"Some hours are remaining to this day," Barbara said after a long while. "Is there anything else you are wanting to do in Rome?" I thought she'd never ask.

"There's a very famous Caravaggio inside this church," I ventured.

"Every Caravaggio is a very famous one, no?"

"*Conversion on the Road to Damascus*," I said. "It's an unusual composition for a religious painting. The backside of a horse dominates the canvas."

"If you already know what it looks like, why must you see it?"

Because I'd studied it in school, written about it, watched the slide-projected image of it bend over Professor Azar's body and now here I was, twenty feet away from it. Because I'd quit my job and come all this way, and who knows when I'd ever have the money to travel like this again. Because I wanted to tell Theo all the things I'd seen and it wouldn't make a good story if I'd sat lazing in the sun on the steps of the Santa Maria del Popolo without bothering to go in and see the *Conversion on the Road to Damascus*. Because, in the painting, Saul is a bad man, a bounty hunter, and, thrown from his horse, he's struck by a vision. Because, in Montreal, I'd dreamt of riding my brown horse, Red, up the Via Appia Antica. A horse on the road to Rome, that was surely a sign.

"I used to have a horse, when I was young," was all I said.

"Ah, *capito*," Barbara said. We got up and went inside.

L eaving is hard, especially places you love, especially early in the morning. Leaving Rome is next to impossible. All roads lead *to* Rome, for one thing. Except for the Grande Raccordo Anulare. The circle highway races round and round the ancient city walls, a battlement of speed and smog. Not even the Vandals, not even Visigoths would have dared invade Rome in this traffic.

My last morning in Rome my hair dryer broke, my coffee burnt and my taxi arrived late. The driver was belligerent about it, and then sped to make up time. The traffic was terrifying. The Raccordo Anulare wound up and pitched us off on to the A12. Which immediately slowed to a crawl, putting the eternal in The Eternal City. You can try to leave Rome all you want to, but long after you've stopped looking over your shoulder, the dome of San Pietro will still be there, floating like a halo at the back of your head.

There's nothing fun about an airport except arriving at your departure gate and hearing the half-forgotten accents of home. *Ben oui.* We were one big, happy, franglais family, until we discovered our flight would be delayed. First for twenty minutes. *Hostie.* Then an hour. *Calice.* A coterie of Québécois, we roamed aimlessly through the duty-free. *Ah, ce sens bon.* Trying on perfume before a transatlantic flight wasn't the best idea I'd ever had. *Mais, c'est pas chère!* By the time we boarded I smelled like a blend of Calvin Klein One and Chanel Number 5, which somehow averaged out to Givenchy.

On the plane, I sat next to a real, live, ancient Roman — an incredibly small old man who had never flown before. He was anxious and without English. His hands were scarred and his arms were brown. At first I thought I might go insane if he didn't stop fiddling with the folding tray in the seatback in front of him, but then the airplane food was such a marvel to him that I softened. It took two stewardesses and an entire Italian-speaking family to convince him that the free headphones were, indeed, free. Finally, gingerly donning them, he looked as if he might weep. The in-flight movie was *My Big Fat Greek Wedding*, an odd choice for Alitalia, I thought, but the old man watched it with such rapture that for the rest of the flight I tried to look at everything as if I'd never seen if before.

On our final descent over Montreal, I spotted our apartment from the air — easily done, as there's a large, green, copper-domed church near us. Considerably smaller than San Pietro, but still. Theo met me at the baggage claim. I was thrilled to see him. Except. Well. Theo doesn't drive, so if he was at the airport I just knew his mother was out there somewhere, circling. I told Theo about how the early morning traffic on the Grande Raccordo Anulare had put the fear of God into me. He tapped his head like they do in the *Astérix and Obélix* comics and said, "These Romans are crazy."

The baggage took forever to emerge, still on Mediterranean time, but all that standing around felt great after eight hours on the plane. I pointed out my ancient Roman seatmate. He looked even smaller now, flanked by two Obélix-sized teens.

"Grandsons," Theo guessed.

"Something skipped a generation," I said.

Finally the baggage carousel sputtered to life. The old man's suitcase was among the first out and, tragi-comically, it was a massive, bulging, brown scuffed thing, cinched by belt and rope. The role of the Obélix-sized grandsons immediately became clear. My suitcase was among the last out. "Is this a suitcase or a bookcase?"

Theo groaned, manoeuvering it toward the door.

It was as hot as Rome outside, and just as humid. But the cars were all enormous — one sure sign I'd left the narrow streets of Rome behind. We found Thérèse idling in a bus-and-taxi-only zone, her bottle-red bouffant gleaming familiarly through the windshield glare. And, upon closer inspection, there was Isaac! Panting and drooling and shedding and wagging in the backseat! The best of all welcome-home surprises.

Between the airport and home we nearly died three times in old-lady-related driving incidents. Every time she stopped short, Isaac fell over. He'd find his feet, she'd take a turn too hard and down he'd go again — yet another episode in the epic struggle between Dog and Centrifugal Force.

Swooping down Clark Street from Little Italy into Mile End Mondial football fan flags festooned every apartment's balcony. The street looked like home but the football felt like Rome. It appeared as if I'd returned on the loudest day of the summer so far, to sticky heat and the stink of mounds of garbage. July 1st moving-day vans parked at traffic-snarling angles. Thérèse double-parked in front of our apartment. Cars honked as they sped past, girls leaned out the windows, waving Portuguese flags.

Thérèse asked me if I'd missed Saint-Urbain Street.

"Yeah," I said. "I missed it a lot."

Our five-and-a-half seemed cavernous after a month in one room plus a kitchenette. I'd forgotten how many books I owned, and how many hot outfits, and cool shoes, and what it was like to drink vodka fresh from the freezer. We drank martinis from actual martini glasses. Theo ordered fried calamari from the Terrasse Lafayette and caught me up on the neighbourhood gossip.

Apparently the Old Greek Lady next door got confused when I first left town; she thought I'd left for good. For weeks, she motherhenned Theo, bringing him banana bread, lettuce from her garden, and one day, inexplicably, a hand-me-down set of floral bed sheets.

"What does she think? I ran off and left you for better linens?"

Finally, Theo enlisted some other Greeks up the street to set the old lady straight. By way of apology, she brought over a fist full of fresh mint.

Naw, whenever their boyfriends went away for the weekend, the tacky anglo girls on the back balcony across from ours invited two loud, shirtless Latino boys over. They sat outside, cracked-wise, drank Coronas and blew cigarette smoke directly into our apartment.

"Where do the boyfriends go?" I wondered.

"Why do they come back?" was Theo's question.

Our old landlord had moved out. A new one had moved in and divided half the backyard into a parking lot. We were excited because at least it wasn't a swimming pool. Our new landlord closely resembled a gorilla. His backyard parking lot was pretty grim. But we'd take it over screaming grandkids any day. Theo and I went out onto the balcony together and solemnly toasted to a summer of quietly parked cars. Isaac nosed his way between our legs to take a look at the yard himself. We all went back in again and I continued my unpacking. Isaac followed me from room to room.

"You've got the dog magnet," Theo said.

"Did you clean up in my office or something?" I asked him.

He admitted that while I was away, Isaac had puked in my home office so many times that huge piles of my stuff had to be thrown away. Now that it was gone I couldn't imagine what I'd been keeping it for. Now that I was back it seemed impossible I'd been away so long. Or that I'd woken up in Rome that morning. Or that this was still the same day.

Leaving is hard, but coming home is so good. Despite the

puke damage, my dog is still the smartest, sweetest, best-looking, best-behaved dog ever. And, in case I haven't mentioned this already, Theo is the best person I know.

It took me days to acclimatize to life without the high whine of two-stroke scooter engines, without the hoards of pick-pockets and tourists and married Italian men asking me to marry them and Japanese tourist men travelling in tight, suit-clad packs, surreptitiously checking out my camera equipment. Theo and I went for an evening stroll. Football fans blocked the sidewalks, watching a game on satellite TV through a jam-packed café's windows. I marvelled at how easy it was to cross the street. "In Rome, the traffic light is merely a suggestion," I said very slowly.

"You're still talking to me as if I don't understand English," Theo said.

"It's so great to walk down the street and understand everything everyone is saying," I said.

"We're on Saint-Viateur Street," Theo said. "Everyone's speaking Italian."

Oh.

Isaac seemed fine to me but I didn't dare say so. Theo was still determined to find a new vet, but too overwhelmed with work to do anything about it just yet, summer being the height of the con-struction season. He was finishing refurbishing an oak-panelled din-ingroom in Outremont that, he said, looked like the inside of a yacht. "I can't imagine how they'll eat in there without getting seasick." Meanwhile, he was in the midst of negotiating a sub-contract to build a custom kitchen in a duplex a few blocks away from our place.

"Careful," I said. "Most accidents happen close to home."

"Maybe we should move."

"We might have to."

Gentrification was creeping ever deeper into our neighbourhood. In the case of this duplex, the immigrant parents had died and the son was sprucing up the place. And not a moment too soon, according to Theo. The kitchen hadn't been remodelled since the fifties. There were melamine-coated chipboard cupboards in the kitchen, and linoleum in the hallway at least three layers deep. "I've seen some ugly wallpaper in my time," Theo said, "but nothing like this."

We tried to take advantage of the few days Theo had off between contracts, but the weather was bad that summer — in ways I wouldn't have expected. Each day dawned hotter than the last. Smog blew in from Toronto. Smoke drifted down from forest fires in northern Quebec. The sky turned acid yellow, and remained that way for days. The back balconies buckled under the weight of the Saint-Urbain Street heat. All the kitchen back doors stood open — sticky arms flung open — imploring in a heat-rashed prayer: Deliver us unto the many gods of Mile End. And, as if in answer, epic thunderstorms rained down on us every evening at rush hour. Isaac hid, for their duration, under my desk.

"The end times are upon us," Theo said, pretending a preacher's solemnity.

"I think this is actually the apocalypse," I said, "only it's happening much slower than we thought it would."

We picked one hell of a summer to stay in the city," Wallace said, the first time I saw him in the dog park after my return.

"It's hotter in Rome," I told him.

"Hot as an *Inferno?*"

"Wow, a Dante joke — not bad for a science teacher!"

"How's the Wonder Dog doing?" Wallace asked, lobbing the orange ball for Isaac. Theo had told Wallace and Dee about the ball-swallowing incident. We told everyone we met, but that didn't make the story any more believable. It didn't help that Isaac was his same old self. Still a champion ball catcher, he came loping back with the orange ball for Wallace to throw, Box nipping at his heels.

"How 'bout you let Box catch one?" I said, but Isaac was already off and running.

"The ball's still in him," I told Wallace, "but he hasn't puked once since I've been back."

"Maybe he was just puking 'cause he missed you."

"Ha, that's what our vet would have us believe. But I'm telling you, if Theo says there's a ball in there, there's a ball in there. We're looking for a new vet, by the way."

"We've started taking Box to a new place on Mont Royal," he said, fumbling in his pockets for a pen.

"Hey, thanks Wallace, this is great," I said, pocketing his chicken-scratched note. He shrugged. The dogs were back with the ball again. This time Wallace faked Isaac out, sent him off in one direction, and then threw the ball the other way for Box.

"How's your summer of festivals going?" I asked.

"Most of the big shows Dee booked tickets for were cancelled at the last minute," he said. "There's a technicians' strike at the Place des Arts." Wallace was a Union man, but under the circumstances he didn't have much sympathy.

"I'm sure there'll be plenty else to see and do," I said.

If anything, there was too much else. Wallace showed me a blood-blister he'd gotten dragging two unwieldy lawn chairs down to Parc Jean Drapeau for the opening ceremonies of the International Fireworks Festival. Dee didn't even sit in hers. "Got to keep moving... mosquitoes," she said. Wallace did his best to avoid noticing a pair of last year's students making out with each other. "Grade eleven chemistry," he quipped to Dee's empty chair.

The fireworks went ahead, despite a heavy mist.

The grass was still damp the next morning, but they packed a picnic anyway and headed over to the Mountain for a free outdoor concert. Wallace thought Schubert until Dee dug the programme out of her purse.

"Schumann," she gloated.

"If the Schu fits..." Wallace murmured. It pained him that the string ensemble couldn't quite fit into the gazebo.

"We don't know any of these people," Dee stage-whispered.

"They're tourists, I guess." Wallace wished he'd paid more attention to all those travel brochures. Summer in the City of Fest wore on. Dee's criticisms became more vocal. Three to five minutes into an event she pronounced it either too amateurish or too ambitious. Wallace couldn't tell ahead of time which she'd think was which. He felt he ought to defend the more valiant efforts: The Model and Mime Fashion Show, for example, and The Unicycle Choir. He quite enjoyed the walking tour of the Kitchen Gardens of Notre-Dame-de-Grâce. Which Dee took as an insult; she spent the rest of that weekend mulching all three-feet square of their perennial bed.

What was worse, Wallace and Dee soon discovered that their next-door neighbours had decided to do decades worth of home renovations that year — new walls, new ceilings, new floors. During the first day of the gutting Wallace went over. Theo answered the door. "Hey Wallace, what are you doing here?" he asked through his dust mask.

"I live next door. What are *you* doing here?"

"The kitchen," Theo said.

"Talk about awkward," I said, when Theo came home with the news.

"Weird that we've seen them so many times in the park and never knew where they lived," he said. He'd dealt with neighbour complaints many times but never from someone he knew personally.

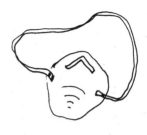

There was no more than the width of a brick wall between the two houses. The vibrations from Theo's belt sander made Dee's grandmother's good china shake. The jolt of the nail gun created chop in the milk in their breakfast cereal.

"Sorry, Wallace," I said, next time I saw him in the park.

"It's not your fault," he said. "Or Theo's. That bastard Howie could have warned us. We've been neighbours for years."

"I guess he thought you'd be on the Grand Manan," I said.

"Maybe. He waited till the end of June."

Isaac seemed to be thriving despite the ball inside of him. We took him to see Box's vet, Dr. Caramel, and she didn't seem that worried about the situation.

"If it's still in there, it's just rolling around in his stomach," she said. "It's round, so it won't hurt him. If he stops pooping, then we have a problem. If his stomach becomes distended, then we have a problem."

Box, on the other hand, was one dusty dog that summer. He barked at nothing, nervous with all the noise next door, and he couldn't take the heat. One night, returning from their late walk, passing through the gate from the back alley into their back yard, Box growled at the fence, convinced of something lurking in Howie's renovation-ravaged yard. Through the hedge, Wallace could just make out a dull gleam atop a heap of torn-out drywall. It was Howie's old toilet, sleek and grey as last year's Grand Manan Blue Heeler.

"It's okay, Box," Wallace said. "Come on inside."

It was hotter inside the house than out. Wallace found Dee in their bedroom watching the weather station on mute — not a good sign.

"High of 19 on the Grand Manan tomorrow," she said. They'd be lucky to get a low of 22 in the city that night.

"Practically a heat wave for down there," Wallace agreed.

Dee started crying chug-a-lug sobs.

"I thought this was what you wanted," Wallace stroked her hair.

"Don't pet me!" she screamed, shrill as a table saw. "I am *not* your dog."

Many people who have never been to Montreal in the summer refuse to believe how hot it gets, because of how cold it gets in the winter. But *we* know. Our literature is drenched in the sweat of our summers. When I read Mordecai Richler's novel, *Son of a Smaller Hero*, in high school in rural Nova Scotia, there was nothing in me that could imagine the high summer Saint-Urbain Street heat. Now Theo and I lived on the same block of Saint-Urbain Street that Mordecai Richler grew up on. *HAVE YOUR DESTINATION IN MIND*. When we went out on our front balcony we relived bodily all Richler's old heat rumours, of old men going crazy and women swooning in the streets. Luckily, no Godzilla-tall caricature of Mordecai Richler loomed over Saint-Urbain Street. My cartoon map had been wrong about that. But tour buses still drove by looking for Mordecai, and upwardly-mobile nostalgics from TMR and Côte-Sainte-Luc still double-parked their BMWs outside Wilensky's at lunchtime, and bought Fairmount bagels by the dozen. We lived closer to Fairmount, but went the distance for Saint-Viateur bagels every time.

Living on Saint-Urbain Street, I was disconcerted to discover that Richler was living in cold dank London when he wrote *Son of a Smaller Hero*, far from the heat of his childhood street. From a story in another book of his, *The Street*, I learned that when Richler returned for a visit to Montreal in the mid-sixties he was shocked by how much the neighbourhood had changed. By changed he meant Greek. Now all the Greeks who lived on our street were ancient.

"Too bad you studied the Romans," Theo said.

Indeed, if I'd focused on the Greeks instead maybe we'd have better relations with our neighbours. To the north of us lived the Greek gods of midnight swimming, divining meaning from the clear waters of their aboveground pool. Strophe and anti-strophe, their call and answer ricocheted, their echos haunting our alley. To the south, the Old Greek Lady and her husband were forever twilight sidewalk-talking under our window. Her hollering and him grunting, they led the neighbours in a chorus, gossip-singing a tin can transistor radio tune.

"Hello, my little baby," the Old Greek Lady called up at Isaac whenever he stuck his nose through our balcony railing into her business. Between him, twitchy as a trigger finger, and her, louder than a car alarm, we had no need for a home security system.

Across the alley a French man — *from France*, as Theo was always sure to point out — waited, quietly, until dinnertime, to aim his trumpet at our apartment. Trumpets are loud and this guy was awful. Theo went over and had words with him, to no avail. A few times we retaliated with better horn players. Chet Baker generally put his efforts into perspective. If he persisted we often resorted to Don Giovanni. In an audio war of attrition, very loud opera almost always wins.

One night we surrendered, at the bugle's call, retreating up the street to the chill interior of Thailande restaurant, to hide, for a meal, from the heat wave's thrall. We splurged on hot food with sides of crispy spinach and marvelled at the waiters' crisp white shirts, lingering for as long as possible over our air-conditioned plates.

 Walking back down Saint-Urbain Street toward home our body temperatures recalibrated to the heat, the night air thick as cream of primordial ooze soup. All the neighbours were outside in their yards, on their front stairs or their balconies. Just sitting there. Waiting. For night to make some difference.

"*Balconville*," Theo said. I thought he'd invented this word until I slipped it into a conversation a week later and was informed that *Balconville* is the title of a David Fennario play so famous that everyone had heard of it except for me. Much to my embarrassment, huge swaths of Quebec culture remained unknown to me.

In French, a "balcony" is a called a *galerie*. Like the visual art gallery, a *galerie* is a site charged with potential, an in-between space, an *entrespace* in which the private unfolds in public display. Summer-long conversations were carried on across our alleyway, climbing over fences, hopscotching from yard to yard. Privacy, oven-baked on an open-faced sandwich, each apartment's *galerie* trained a curious, opera-glass eye upon its neighbouring loge. The sun tanning, the dinner guests, the gardening, garbage and household repairs. Up the street, the neighbours' empty pool gurgled above ground — a waiting sound — restless as nest-bound birds.

Even in the evening, the hardwood floor felt too hot for feet too swollen for shoes. Our bare feet left footprints on the dust dishevelled dim hallway's worn floorboards. Dog hair clumped in the corners like tumbleweeds waiting for a breeze. The dog lay on his side on the floor; all four legs stuck out flat as a hieroglyph.

"The dog appears to be broken," Theo said.

"Either that or he's an Egyptian."

It was too hot to sleep. The airless city sat on edge. On the back balcony's ledge of tepid dusk, I slumped, my limp flip-flop dangling from a painted toe — nails chipped. Said flip-flop fell free — dropped into the yard below, into a statuary of neighbours. Undisturbed, too hot to move, the neighbours didn't look up. Only their voices rang out — a multi-lingual choir of staccato airs and grievances.

In the morning the air was cooler outside than in, wood smoke from Saint-Viateur Bagels' endless ovens anointed another day. Another scorcher. Sesame seeds smiled in the sidewalk's cracked teeth.

We hardly saw Dee anymore. Each time we saw Wallace and Box, Box looked more bedraggled. Theo finished up his part of the construction next door to them as fast as possible but then other sub-contractors moved in. The tile cutter guy worked glacier slow. The hardwood floor was so scored and scarred that it needed three passes with the sander. The noise and the dust, and then the fumes from each new coat of stain, varnish, and paint waged war on everyone's nerves.

By the end of the summer, Dee had kicked Wallace out.

"It's not me, it's you," she told him.

We urged Wallace to keep in mind that none of it had actually been his fault. *She* was the one who had wrecked the Grand Manan for them; *she* was the one who had insisted on staying in the city for the summer. He hadn't had a thing to do with the strike at Place des Arts. And the heat wave, the forest fire haze, and Howie's ill-timed home renovations — those were all acts of God, weren't they?

Wallace took an apartment, a small place close to the school where he taught. Walking to and from work everyday he quickly lost ten pounds, and kept it off by not learning how to cook. He ate steamed vegetables and Uncle Ben's Instant Rice and slept like a baby after he discovered that he'd been relegated to the wrong side of the bed during all those years with Dee.

Dee kept the house. She tried to keep Box too, but in the end Wallace got him every other week. He tried not to take it personally, but it turned out that Box hated linoleum. Wallace's new place was slick with it. On the weeks when Box was with him, Wallace had to cover his floors with cardboard.

Box suffered, shuttled back and forth like a child between the house and the apartment. He began to show his age. His winter coat didn't grow in thick enough; he became yippy and whiny. "I think you get that from your mother, Box," Wallace said, attempting to make light of the situation.

On an evening walk during Dee's week with Box, Dee stopped on the corner to talk to a man Box had never met before. Box wandered off toward Wallace's. He knew the way all right, but he'd never made the trip alone. Crossing Bernard Street, Box was hit by a car. His injuries were mostly internal.

"Not for love or money," Dr. Caramel said, and shook her head.

Wallace and Dee took Box home in a box, and buried him near the boxwood hedge in what was now Dee's backyard. The accident was Wallace's fault too, obviously.

"You turned that dog against me," Dee sobbed.

Wallace attacked the late-winter, frost-hard dirt with his shovel.

Two months later, Dee's lawyer informed Wallace that Dee had decided to sell the house. It was good news, really — she was moving to Moncton. They all took pity on Wallace at work. That was the hardest part. He couldn't come out and tell them that he didn't mind that his wife had left him, could he?

It was his dog he missed.

If Isaac missed Box, we couldn't tell. He was happy about spring, but not about the slush. He hadn't passed the ball, as our old vet had said he would. We had more confidence in his new vet, Dr. Caramel. She had said to call her if we noticed any new complications. Isaac still puked once in a while, but not enough to alarm us. He seemed to be moving kind of slow, for spring. I wasn't sure if that was a good enough reason to take him to the vet. "It sounds like the beginning of a Yiddish joke: Doctor, doctor — my dog's moving kind of slow." Fortunately it was time for Isaac's vaccinations so we had an excuse to take him to see Dr. Caramel.

Dr. Caramel was running late. By the time it was Isaac's turn he'd befriended three black kittens and a puffy black puppy. His bias toward animals the same colour as him continued to embarrass us, but at least he didn't discriminate against size, shape or species.

"He's lost a little weight," Dr. Caramel said. "Is he still throwing up?"

"Mostly only when he eats garbage in the alley."

"Sounds reasonable," she said. "But if you don't mind, I'd like to see him back here in a few weeks." On our way out the door she said, "Hey, someone showed up yesterday with a stray puppy.

Needs a home. Know anyone who might be interested?" If we had a puppy for every time we've been asked that... but for once, I happened to know of someone who was short a dog.

"We might," I said, and asked if her office could keep the puppy overnight while we sorted things out.

"What are you thinking?" Theo demanded as soon as we were out on the sidewalk. I laid my plan on him. He was against it.

"People have to pick their own dogs," he said.

"We didn't pick Isaac, he picked us."

"It's too big a decision, Simone. And it's none of our business." I reminded him that if Julie had minded her own business then we might never have met. Eventually he relented. The next day we called and the puppy was still there. We walked down to Dr. Caramel's office to pick her up, then walked another ten blocks up and over to Wallace's, taking turns carrying her, still agonizing over whether or not we were doing the right thing.

Wallace answered the door with a wad of newspapers under his arm.

"Are we disturbing you?" I asked, hiding behind Theo.

"No, no, not at all. You're saving me from the Arts & Leisure section. The previews of this year's summer festivals are perky enough to make you puke."

We edged our way into his meagre hallway.

"We figured it's been long enough," I said and handed him the puppy.

"What's this?" Wallace asked. A black puffball with blue eyes.

"You look like a man who doesn't know what to do with a baby. Go on, set her down."

"Female," Wallace said, and set her down. The pup didn't seem to mind the linoleum. Her toenails click-clacked, cautious as a first-timer in high heels.

Theo took a look around Wallace's apartment with a renovator's expert eye. The place was clean, orderly and bland. Like he'd been waiting for something.

"How you getting on?" I asked him.

The pup tiptoed up to smell his pant leg.

"Gingerly," he said.

That was his name for the dog in his head: Ginger Lee. He called her Ginger in public — a Golden Retriever's name — all wrong for her black hair and blue eyes. Ginger wasn't ginger at all. She grew fast, and ran faster than any dog out there.

"What's your dog's name?" they'd ask him in the dog park.

"Ginger," he'd say with a smile.

"Ginger, eh? And what's your name, Fred?" So everyone and their dog started calling him Fred. Wallace had never had a nickname before. Everybody asked him, "What kind of dog is that?" He answered, "Huskyblacklab," like it was all one word.

"It's a good combo," I said. "Huskies like to run dead ahead, but Labradors are retrievers; they'll always come back to you."

Wallace squinted across the park to where Ginger was playing catch with Theo and Isaac. She intercepted Isaac's ball, trotted over to Wallace with it in her mouth and deposited it at his feet. Wallace threw the slobber-slick ball in a park-long lob and the whole pack of them chased. He and Ginger Lee were ready. This year, the dog park. Next year, summer on the Grand Manan.

The summer of Ginger Lee, Theo decided once and for all to quit working renovation and focus full time on furniture design. The Wallace and Dee renovation hell had been bad enough but then Adrian got an eviction notice. I told Theo, "You'd better not have anything to do with the renovation of his

old place — we'd never hear the end of it."

"I already turned the job down," he said.

Then the landlord of the building next door died. Her son flew in from Toronto to assess the situation. His first move was to evict the Old Greek Lady and her husband. They'd lived in that ground-floor flat for 23 years. You'd have thought I'd be happy to see her go. I'd complained about her often enough: all day, every day, cursing at her husband, blabber-mouthing with neighbours and nonsense chattering at the alley kids, and cats, and birds. All that spring, we watched the discarded detritus of her life accumulate in the back alley. Passers-by rifled through her children's old school textbooks in boxes marked: *free / à donner*. The bottom drawer of her rain-swollen commode became home to a litter of kittens. The stuff she couldn't bear to throw out, she foisted off on neighbours. We got a second appalling set of floral bed sheets and a painting of a Grecian isle.

July 1st, moving day, half the street turned out to see the Old Greek Lady and her husband leave. One look at the moving van and her Siamese cat went missing. It resisted capture all summer, even as the apartment was gutted and retrofitted. It turned out that I'd much rather listen to an old lady cursing in Greek than a 7 AM tile-cutter or a supper time belt-sander. Theo bet the new owner would live in the new apartment for exactly one year, as law required, before he flipped it. Whoever moved in after all the Old Greek Lady's stories were erased from the place would pay at least triple her rent.

Mile End was changing. We could be next.

Our newest not-yet neighbours left a letter in every mailbox on our block warning us all that they'd be renovating, apologizing in advance of the noise. Their note didn't mention that there'd be trucks blocking the alley for four months. We sat in our kitchen and listened to their contractors cursing between bursts of jack-hammer and band saw, and mourned the passing of what used to be. Their back fence used to have an ancient wooden door in it, sagging blue, askew, amidst a retinue of vines clinging to crumbling cinderblocks, guarding an oasis of lazy Brown-Eyed-Susans. Now there's a backhoe clawing after a basement. The first time we met these new neighbours was in the back alley by the blue door. The ground was still frozen. They threw a stick for our dog and told us how they'd decided to buy the place. "We fell in love with the garden," they said. Every day since, we've walked the dog through the mud from the hole they've dug and remembered this story.

This is our back alley. This is a walk we walk every day. It's a long block. Five minutes from bottom to top. Six if you walk slowly. Seven if you walk as if intent on studying every scent. A dog's age if you're sniffing for stories.

Maybe you've met our dog. He knows people that we don't. One time, at one of Adrian's elaborate dinner parties, we overheard a man we'd never met before talking about The Dog with the Orange Ball.

We said: "That's our dog!"

He said: "That's crazy!"

He's never even seen our dog, but his daughter knows the sound of our dog's tags. He lifts her up so she can watch The Dog with the Orange Ball running up the alley. We've since glimpsed her pixie head peeking over their high fence.

We throw the orange ball and our dog brings it back to us.

We throw the orange ball and our dog brings it back.

We throw the orange ball and he chases and sometimes we miss. Three times up and three times down, day after day, and it's hard to say how many orange balls we've sent sailing over cinderblock fences into thigh-high tomatoes or sunk into knee-deep snow. Sorry if we've ever snuck into your yard in an attempt to retrieve the ball *du jour*. Dogs know nothing of private property.

Tess wrote from Vermont to say that at long last Earl had finished building their house. They were all moved in and ready for guests. Theo said we had to go. I had a writing deadline. "But after that," I said. Thérèse couldn't decide if she wanted to come with us or not. We helped her decide by suggesting we'd better check the house out first, make sure it was *propre*.

"Now that there's a house to stay in, they'll be inundated with visitors!" Theo said.

Tess's letter included a drawing of the new house. Apparently it had seventeen windows, all on one side. Tess was home-schooling little Daniel. She wrote that he had quite the artistic side.

"Maybe he'll be an architect," I said, taping the seventeen-windowed house drawing to our fridge.

"Well, at least he has the homesteading to fall back on," Theo said.

"Hey, watch it, mister. I studied homesteading and I turned out just fine."

"*Touché.*"

My desire to leave farm life behind had merged perfectly with my unwillingness to ever enter the full-time corporate workforce again, motivating me to hunt down freelance writing gigs with new ferocity, to propose stories of interest to me, to invent opportunities for myself where previously there'd been none. Since returning from Rome I'd written about the modern city relentlessly. One short article called "The New Empire" had been published in a travel magazine. I had no qualms about capitalizing on my corporate experiences either. I'd pitched a long non-fiction piece called "Undercover Operation: One Net-Worker Tells All," and was finishing up a catalogue essay for a New Media art exhibit set to open in Montreal in the fall. As soon as that essay was done we borrowed Julie's car, once again, and drove down to Vermont via our favourite Champlain Islands route.

Isaac was deeply suspicious of cars. Too often he'd been subjected to nerve-wracking rides in the city with Theo's mother at the wheel. It was a lot easier to convince him to climb into the backseat if Thérèse was nowhere in sight. If I was driving, in his experience, we usually ended in the great outdoors, a park, or something fun. Inner city stop-and-go gave him motion sickness, but once we were on the highway he was all right. We worried, as we slowed for the border crossing, that Isaac would puke all over the back seat. He stood up, shaky, and stared out the rear window, looking back at the way we came. When we handed the border guard our passports and Isaac's vaccination records, the border guard called out Isaac's name. Isaac's ears triangulated. He turned to look at the border guard with his trademark tilt of the head. Irrefutable proof that we were who we said we were.

Sadly, there was no one named Hayes buried in the South Hero Island Cemetery. We posed Isaac for a photo next to a Newton tombstone instead. He heard Tess and Earl's dog before we did, and struggled to stand in the backseat. The minute Theo opened the back door for him he leapt out, barking.

"He doesn't usually bark like that," Theo said, intercepting a flying leap hug from little Daniel who was a full foot taller than the last time we'd seen him.

"He's pissed off that we never told him about Vermont before," I said, hugging Tess. "This is the biggest dog park he's ever seen."

The finished house looked like it had been there for years already.

"They don't build them like this *en ville*," Earl gloated to Theo.

"No sir, they do not," Theo said, stroking a dowel-framed door he'd built, looking for cracks or warps. There were none.

To celebrate the new house, I suggested Theo and I treat Tess, Earl and little Daniel to a dinner out, anywhere they liked. "Shouldn't we stay *in* the house, now that it's done?" Theo asked.

Tess screamed, "Thai food!" and ran upstairs to get dressed. Apparently a new Thai restaurant had opened recently, in a rundown little mill town a thirty-five minute drive from their homestead on the high plains, downhill all the way.

"How did you hear about this place?" I asked Tess as we were seated.

"Are you kidding? Something as exotic as a Thai restaurant opens up around here and within days the whole North East Kingdom knows about it."

The waiter claimed to have never heard of crispy spinach, but the *pad thai* was passable and the *mee krob* really quite good.

"Microbe?" Earl looked like he'd rather eat his hand.

Tess refused to let any of us eat with chopsticks, because they looked too much like cigarettes. She'd vowed to give up smoking once the house was finished. "Smoking is the only thing I miss about the trailer," she said.

Daniel spent most of the meal mesmerized by the fish tank. Veil-tailed goldfish, mauve-bellied butterfly fish, and about five bucks worth of silver dollars swam in simple, blue-lit wonder.

"He's never seen live fish before," Tess said.

"That's really what they look like?" he kept asking her.

"There are lots of fish in the sea," Earl grinned. Note to self: buy this landlocked kid a book about the ocean.

The waiter brought a plastic cup full of crayons over for Daniel. He drew fish all over his paper placemat. The waiter brought him another one. He drew a dog we thought looked a lot like Isaac. "Is that for us?" Theo asked him. "No," he said. But Tess slipped it to me under the table as we were leaving the restaurant. When Theo, Isaac and I got back to Montreal we reconsidered the drawn dog's resemblance to Isaac. Little Daniel had already known plenty of dogs in his short lifetime. If he'd wanted to draw our dog, he would have. At the Thai restaurant he'd only had eyes for the fish tank.

"This dog looks fishy to me," Theo said.

I taped it to the fridge anyway, next to the seventeen-windowed house.

E veryone I'd ever known in Montreal showed up for the *vernissage* of The New Media exhibit that accompanied my catalogue essay. Julie brought flowers and a crew of our old friends from the corporate world.

"Wow Simone, I didn't know you wrote," said a guy from Product Marketing. I'd worked with him for over a year and the fact that I wrote was the least of all the things he didn't know about me.

"I always wanted to do that, you know, just stay home and write," mused a senior interface designer who made more money a year than Theo and I ever had combined, even when I was working.

"That your BMW SUV out front?" I asked him.

"Yeah," he said.

"Sell that, and you could afford to stay home and write full-time for about two years."

Vita came, flanked by a fresh crew of History of Hellenistic Sculpture students.

"How did you convince them New Media counts as Art History?"

"It will be eventually," she said. She introduced me to her students as "the author" and referred to me as "a colleague." I hoarded these phrases with pride.

My former Technology in Contemporary Art professor, butted in on my conversation with Vita to stutter his praises. "B-b-b-b-b-bravo," he said, proffering his copy of the catalogue for me to sign.

"If only he'd thought as highly of my efforts in his class," I said to Vita when, at last, he had moved on.

"Doesn't he deserve some credit for dragging you into the twenty-first century?"

"No, that would be his fault," I said, pointing toward Theo. He waved and came over. We watched as Wallace stood in the foyer and read the catalogue cover to cover before venturing into the gallery. He was looking even more like a high school teacher than usual. Reading glasses on a string must come standard with every Bachelor of Education degree.

"I'm having an if-only-they-could-see-me-now moment," I told Theo.

"Who are you thinking of?"

"Mostly people who I'm glad aren't here."

I had sent a copy of the catalogue to my parents. So far, I'd heard no word back from them. My grade twelve English teacher would be drunk on free *vernissage* wine by now. The Vaughn kids would bring their kids, plunk them down in front of the video art and call it television.

"I have been thinking a lot about my old friend Isaac lately," I said. "Do you think there's a list somewhere of contact info for people in the Navy?"

"We could ask the Internet," Theo said. "I bet it will know."

Adrian showed up late, with an incredibly tall accordion player who spoke in perplexing non-sequiturs. He and Adrian argued all evening over which room of the exhibit I ought to stand in. "Video projection is not your best light," Adrian assured me. And then left without saying good-bye.

After the *vernissage*, Theo headed home to walk Isaac. I went drinking with the leftovers of this weird mix of worlds — me, and some of my friends' closest friends. Somehow we wound up at a foul-smelling, not-quite-dimly-lit-enough bar you wouldn't want to walk into even during the day on a crumbling block of Avenue du Parc. Someone in our group had a dog, a yippy little thing that hung out under our table all evening, looking for all the world like the mangy ghost of Trixie, the murdered Vaughn dog.

At three in the morning we stumbled out on the *terrasse*. Drunk, but not as drunk as all that. Waiting for all the good-byes to be said, I leaned down to pat the dog — out of sympathy more than anything — it was so ugly. The little beast bit me. I was shocked. I mean literally — I went into shock and passed out. When I regained consciousness, I had no idea where I was or that I was laid out flat on my back. Familiar faces floated in front of me. "What are you doing here?" I asked them collectively.

The dog's owner was a dancer. She informed me that, in her professional opinion, not only had I fallen quite gracefully, but I had also done so in the way least likely to result in injury to myself. Which did nothing to stop my hand from swelling, throbbing and bleeding slightly from three big, ugly welts. Impressive wounds from such a little dog's bite. The ghost of Trixie, seeking her revenge.

The dancer and her vile companion walked me home. I woke Theo. He was furious, not least of all because it was almost 4 AM. "Did you ask if the dog had its shots?" He demanded, disinfecting and dressing my wounds.

"I'll call the owner in the morning," I promised.

In the morning my head hurt more than my hand. Theo insisted on disinfecting again anyway, the rubbing alcohol stinging, clearing my head. "The hair of the dog that bit me," I said.

"If that dog's vicious it should be put down," Theo said.

"That would be overkill," I said, explaining my ghost of Trixie theory.

I was just about to start making some phone calls to track down the dog's owner, to ask if its rabies shots were up to date, when Adrian called me to tell me an ex of his had just called to tell him he'd seen me seen passed out drunk in front of a notorious coke bar at 3 AM.

"I wasn't drunk," I said. "I got bit by a dog."

"That's not what I heard."

The first version of a story is the one most people cling to.

The bite wounds burned and itched all week. No matter how much I didn't pick at the scabs there were bound to be scars.

E arly Sunday morning, Isaac had diarrhoea, stopped eating and started throwing up water and bile. Monday, he stopped puking, but didn't start eating. Tuesday morning, still no eating, and he started twitching and getting stiff in the legs. By the end of his early walk he could barely walk. We called Dr. Caramel's clinic. She said she was booked solid, but that we should bring him in right away anyway. I called Julie at work. "Please don't ask why," I said, "but can I borrow your car right this minute?"

"Is Isaac okay?"

"Where are you parked?"

"Wow, that bad? All right. Waverly, just south of Saint-Viateur. Call me when you can, okay?"

By the time we got Isaac to the vet, he looked like he was a hundred years old. Theo carried him into Dr. Caramel's exam room and set him down on the concrete floor. He stood splay-legged and shaking.

Theo reminded her that there was a ball inside the dog.

She said, "I know there is, I believe you. But this is way worse than that. The ball wouldn't cause stiffness in the legs like this." As if to illustrate, Isaac's front legs buckled beneath him. Theo let out a sound that I'd never heard him make before, and hid his face in his hands. Outside the exam room, a little dog was barking and a power saw was whining. Dr. Caramel's clinic was under renovation. She would have a surgery and an X-ray machine on site by next week. Not soon enough for us. Her phones were ringing and her staff were scrambling to manage the waiting room backlog while Dr. Caramel waited patiently for Theo and I to get it through our thick heads that our dog was dying.

"Your dog is as sick as a dog can get," she said.

Isaac scrambled to stand like a calf with foot-and-mouth disease would. Theo couldn't look at him. Theo the Calm was losing his shit. Some hard, farm girl part of me kicked in. Hard as the part of my father that had castrated bull calves, slaughtered steers, beheaded chickens and dipped bare hands into writhing hives of honeybees. I stepped around Isaac to where Theo sat slumped at the exam table.

"Suck it up," I said, very close to his ear so Dr. Caramel wouldn't hear. "This dog needs both of us to get it together right this minute."

Dr. Caramel never once pretended she knew what was wrong with Isaac. She suspected cancer of the spine, but she would need X-rays to be sure. We'd need to go elsewhere for those. We didn't know if Isaac would live through the night. We had some big decisions to make. Tests to take, results to wait for, scenarios to consider. Dr. Caramel told us how much each procedure would cost and what it would mean for the dog. "We don't want him to suffer," we said over and over, even though he was clearly in agony. What we meant was, we didn't want to spend thousands for painful procedures from which he might never recover. What we meant was, we didn't want him to suffer for our guilt. We had a euthanasia conversation. We decided we had to know what was wrong with him before taking that step. We agreed to leave Isaac at Dr. Caramel's clinic overnight, and hope she could get him in somewhere else for X-rays in the morning.

She put him on antibiotics and asked if we'd mind going to the drug store down the street to fill the prescription for a narcotic painkiller patch to get him through the night.

"If I send someone from my staff it will back everything up even further over here," Dr. Caramel explained. Her waiting room was full to overflowing, thanks to Isaac's unscheduled emergency. At the drug store the pharmacist asked Theo for his health care card. Theo looked at him blankly. "*C'est pour un chien*," he said.

Once the painkiller patch was attached to a shaved area on the back of Isaac's neck, he calmed down considerably. It was a relief to see him sedated. "Could you prescribe a few more of those?" we implored.

"Go home and get some rest," Dr. Caramel said. "I'll call you if there's news."

I drove us home slowly through the streets of Mile End; up Waverly, down Clark, around and around looking for parking. Each street, street corner, street sign, fire hydrant, tree, shrub, fence post, garbage can and curb was haunted by Isaac.

"If he dies," I said, "we'll have to move."

"He's not going to die," Theo said.

"He might."

"Let's try not to think about that."

"We can't not think about it. We can't make decisions unless we think about it."

"What I mean is, I'm not ready to give up on him yet."

"I'm not giving up on him."

"I know you're not…"

"I'm just saying, we have to mentally prepare ourselves for the possibility."

We went around and around like this, instinctively sticking to the relative safety of semantic arguments, rather than plunging into the deep waters of wild speculation. Dr. Caramel called at 6 PM to say the results of one set of lab tests were in. The good news was, it wasn't meningitis. The bad news was, the lab said the lymphoma tests would take five days. If it was lymphoma, Isaac wouldn't live that long. Around 8 PM, Dr. Caramel called again, this time with something more concrete: she'd convinced a clinic in NDG to take Isaac for X-rays first thing in the morning.

"Better make sure we can keep Julie's car another day," Theo said. Good point. I dialled her number. As soon as she answered I realized there was no way I could tell her how sick Isaac was over the phone. I decided to walk over and talk to her in person. An evening walk without the dog felt so wrong that by the time I got to Julie's I was a mess. Her front door was open. I walked in and locked myself in her bathroom. Sobs and dry heaves. She called Theo. He came over and told her everything in quiet French. And then took me home.

E arly the next morning, we drove down to Dr. Caramel's clinic, bracing ourselves for what we might find there. We sat on the front steps and waited. The receptionist arrived first. She hurried in ahead of us to check on Isaac; peering into the window of the room he'd spent the night in. We could tell from the look on her face that he was still alive. Dr. Caramel came in a few minutes later. She gave him a once-over. He wasn't doing any better. He couldn't get much worse. Theo carried him out to the car. On our way out, Dr. Caramel handed us an extra towel, which we accepted as a talisman to protect us against whatever was coming next.

They were no-nonsense at the NDG clinic. Dr. Caramel had briefed Dr. Larkin on the phone. He ushered us into the X-ray room right away. Isaac was so stiff in the legs the X-ray technicians had a hard time getting him into position. The first X-ray showed, without a shadow of a doubt, that there was no cancer of the spine. "We would see small holes in the bones here," they said, pointing. They moved Isaac into a different position, working patiently, gently, quietly. His eyes followed their every move.

In the past twenty-four hours we'd heard every possible diagnosis, from lymphoma to meningitis to acute rheumatoid arthritis to liver cancer and lots of other even worse sounding things that I couldn't remember the names of because I kept blocking them from my mind. Now that most of those had been ruled out we didn't know what we were looking for anymore, which terrified us. We pored over each new X-ray as if we were experts. The definitive moment came when Dr. Larkin looked at one of Isaac's abdominal X-rays and said, "That's totally bizarre."

Well, then, we knew we were on to something.

"See this void," Dr. Larkin said, his finger tracing a large empty shape inside the dog. "It's fluid, gastric juices probably. His stomach is severely distended. But we're not seeing it from the outside because he's lost so much weight."

"Okay, so what causes a severely distended stomach?" we wanted to know.

"It could be a number of things. His intestines could be twisted, or possibly blocked by a foreign object that's not showing up on the X-ray," he said.

"Well, we know there's a foreign object in him! It's a ball!!"

We agreed to exploratory surgery. It would have to wait a few hours, though. Isaac needed to be re-hydrated first. And Dr. Larkin needed lunch. "Can I bring you two some food?" he asked us. "Slice of pizza maybe?" The NDG Clinic was our new favourite place on earth.

Waiting was the worst part. We soon learned that the best

place to do your waiting is down at dog level. We sat on the towel Dr. Caramel had given us, on the concrete floor of the surgery, where Isaac and three or four other pre- and post-op cats and dogs were laid out on blanket and towel pallets. Dr. Larkin and his assistants stepped over and around them as they worked. "We like to keep them with us," one assistant explained.

The animals on staff at NDG clinic made the waiting easier. Kiwi the parrot talked to the dental machinery. Molly the bow-legged mini-Daschund marched around minding everyone's business. We also discovered that the NDG clinic runs an un-official animal shelter. There's a room off the surgery full of perfectly good pets. People bring them in to be put down. Dr. Larkin just can't do it. Honey the sexy tabby cat had been there long enough to earn wandering around privileges. She sat with her back to Isaac, but very close to him, for hours on end. The human staff was amazed by this.

"Honey's afraid of animals," they said.

"It must be hell for her, living here then," I said. I hadn't had a cat since Feather of the Fairies. Honey's dog-like stoicism might have convinced us to adopt her, under other circumstances.

"Sorry, Honey," Theo said. "We've got our hands full."

M id-afternoon, Dr. Larkin prescribed us some fresh air. "We'll go into surgery at four," he said. "Come back then." " YOU WANT TO GO FOR A WALK? " Theo asked me.

He tucked the bath towel Dr. Caramel had given us under his arm, just in case. I had a plastic bag in my back pocket. Some dog preparedness habits are hard to shake. We ventured down Sherbrooke Street far enough to purchase double lattés and then, like a sling-shot elastic contracting, we scurried back toward the clinic.

"We can't go back in yet," I said, looking at my watch. "We've only been gone eighteen minutes." We still had an hour and a half left to wait.

" YOU WANT TO GO TO THE PARK? " Theo asked, pointing to a green space the next block over. We spread out the towel on a grassy spot near a fountain. It was sunny, which was surprising to me. It was cold, I thought, but then Theo wanted to move the blanket into a shadier spot because he was too hot. In the shade, he shivered. Stupid-tired, stressed and stuck in a difficult-decision-instant-replay feedback loop, we shifted and squirmed and stood and stretched and fidgeted, second-guessing ourselves until we were practically out of our minds.

"I guess I should start considering the possibility that he might make it through this," I said after a long while.

"Yes, you should." The way Theo said this made me realize. All this time that I'd been steeling myself for the worst, he'd been hoping for the best.

For the rest of our park purgatory we sat still as animals on guard.

The surgery started at 4 PM as scheduled. Finally, something scheduled. The operating room had a window but we couldn't watch. At 4:10 one of Dr. Larkin's surgical assistants came out with a glass decanter full of pinkish-yellow liquid that she tried to hide from us even as she poured it down the sink. At 4:14 she came out again. This time the decanter was only two-thirds full.

"Stomach fluids?" I asked her. Theo blanched.

"Gastric acid," she said. "A litre and a half."

No wonder he was puking. No wonder he couldn't walk.

At 4:18 Dr. Larkin's assistant came out again. "You're going to want to see this," she said.

"Are you sure?" Theo asked her.

We willed ourselves over to the operating room window. Dr. Larkin showed us a distinctly ball-shaped section of small intestine. Just like in the cartoons, when a snake swallows a rabbit and you see the rabbit shape — ears and all — passing through the snake. He really is a cartoon character, our dog.

By 4:20, the ball was out of the dog. The assistant washed it off and handed it to us. It was a hard, black, India rubber ball. A small dog's ball. Theo tested it. It still had its bounce. Passing it back and forth between us Theo and I told the story of the dog swallowing the ball to all the people who worked at the clinic.

"Our old vet told us it would break apart in his stomach," I said. Theo gave the ball another bounce. The NDG Clinic staff collectively shook their heads.

Dr. Caramel called while Isaac was still in surgery. "I'm so sorry I didn't take your story about the ball more seriously," she said.

"It's not your fault," I said. "Our old vet didn't take it seriously, so we didn't take it seriously enough either... The story's a whole lot more believable now that we're holding the ball."

"You're holding the ball? How big is it?"

"Well, it's larger than a small intestine."

One of the many things we discovered during this ordeal is that animal clinics go through vast numbers of towels and blankets every day. They rely on donations. We vowed to spread the word on this so people know — everyone has old towels and blankets. And just about any animal clinic or shelter or hospital will find them useful. Another thing we realized is that vets treat people too — for shock and fear and indecision and emotion. A whole extended community of people helped us make the long string of difficult decisions that eventually saved Isaac's life. The amazing women who work at the NDG Clinic were honest and human and fast. They brought us snacks and told us jokes all the while working their asses off, doing six or seven surgeries the day we were there.

An older woman with a gimpy leg came in looking to adopt a cat just after Isaac came out of his surgery. He was lying on the floor on yet another pallet of donated towels and blankets, flopping around sporadically, the way we'd seen other dogs do after their surgeries earlier in the day. "Do you have any pets already?" we asked her. No, she did not. So we introduced the woman to Honey the sexy tabby cat, singing her praises. Honey strutted and struck pretty poses. When the woman with the gimpy leg stepped over Isaac on her way out, clutching Honey in her arms, he jerked his head up to look at them both, and then flopped down again with an incredible sigh. We felt certain this was a good omen.

I saac recovered amazingly quickly, once the ball was out of him. He spent the night at the NDC Clinic. We took him home the next day. He looked years younger.

"He looks like a million bucks," one neighbour said.

"More like twelve hundred," we said.

" NO BALL ," we had to tell him at first. No ball, no running and quite a few stitches. Once he got his stitches out he got his orange ball back. Once he got his orange ball back, he got his bounce back.

Now Isaac's famous on our street. He's the dog who swallowed the ball. It was a small dog's ball. And Isaac is medium, that's what the alley kids say. A medium dog with an orange ball. And we are his people. Isaac walks Theo and me up and down the alley three times a day. Toenails clicking on cracked concrete. Trail zigzagging, long tail wagging, long tongue lolling, dog tags clacking. Ears open, eyes darting, nose to the ground.

Plastic bags protruding from our pockets, we follow in his wake, braving the seasons, the wind in our ears. We wade through the slush and shit of each spring. We scavenge our way through heaps of moving-day garbage, cut our feet on broken glass and sneeze at renovation rubble. We snap off spring sprigs of low-slung lilacs and pluck blackberries through diamond-back fences. We pilfer other dogs' balls from other dogs' yards; run wild past wildflowers, weeds and fallen leaves, so free we set the whole alley barking.

Theo and I try to see things from the dog's eye view, to read between these long lines of peeling-paint fences spray-painted with bright abstractions and draped with trailing vines. We walk as if we own the place, intent on studying every scent. Chasing stories changing from minute to minute, we never want the alleyway to end.

ACKNOWLEDGEMENTS

Some portions of *Words the Dog Knows* have previously appeared, often in very different forms, in: *The New Quarterly*, *Geist*, and *The Knight Literary Journal*, on *NthPosition.com*, on my blog, *Lapsus Linguae*, and in my electronic literature projects *in absentia*, *Entre Ville* and *How I Loved the Broken Things of Rome*, all of which can be found at <luckysoap.com>. For their support in the creation of those works I gratefully acknowledge the Canada Council for the Arts, Conseil des arts et des lettres du Québec, Conseil des Arts de Montréal, OBORO, DARE-DARE, The Playwrights' Workshop Montreal, The Caravan Collective, The Corporation of Yaddo, The Ucross Foundation, Caldera, The Vermont Studio Center, The Orchard Group and The Banff Centre (for the Arts).

Most of *Words the Dog Knows* was written in Montreal, between November 2007 and August 2008. Andy Brown, you tricked me. Thank you for teaching me the word "novel." Thanks Maya Merrick, for aiding and abetting; we'll always have Rome. Editorial thanks also to Dr. Boyce, for chasing the ball of language, and Nora Maynard, for your long-distance stamina. Thanks to all the teachers. Cabrini Kelly, that lesson on setting in grade nine English has really come in handy. Ingrid Bachmann, you are a great artist. Kai and Glenn, you inspire us by loving and living so well. Dave Jones, you taught me brevity. Julie Gagné, in your memory we strive to live better. Gladys Fleishman, I wish you'd lived to see the day. OBORO, you are my art family. Trautz Family, your hearts and minds have made Cabot Plains the best place on earth to write. Thanks Amy Hempel, for underlining the good parts. Karen Russell, for making me funnier. Jason Camlot, for rhyming all the timing always chiming in with your support. Will Richards, patron of the arts. Lisa Vinebaum, for the tomato juice: u r our hero. Denise, *merci pour tout ce que vous faites pour nous.* Roxane Archambault-Vermette, for the drawing. Barbaraina, *cicerone mia.* Dr. Judith, Dr. Allen and Dr. Elkin for curing people too. Thanks to all the dogs: Mingus, Zig-Zig, Cartier, Bernadette, Lucy, Lulu, Lola and Nashua, Salomé, Chester and Hazel, Roxy, Renaldo, Clifford, Itchy and Scratchy, Brixton, Danny and Trixie. Isaac, thank you for choosing us. Stéphane Vermette, you are the best person I know.

J. R. CARPENTER GREW UP ON A FARM IN NOVA SCOTIA AND HAS LIVED IN MONTREAL SINCE 1990. SHE IS A TWO-TIME WINNER OF THE CBC QUEBEC SHORT STORY COMPETITION AND A WEB ART FINALIST IN THE DRUNKEN BOAT PANLITERARY AWARDS 2006. HER ELECTRONIC LITERATURE HAS BEEN PRESENTED INTERNA-TIONALLY. HER SHORT FICTION HAS BEEN BROADCAST ON CBC RADIO, TRANSLATED INTO FRENCH, AND ANTHOLOGIZED IN *LE LIVRE DE CHEVET, SHORT STUFF, LUST FOR LIFE* AND *IN OTHER WORDS*, AND HAS APPEARED IN JOURNALS INCLUDING *GEIST, THE NEW QUARTERLY* AND *MATRIX*. SHE CURRENTLY SERVES AS PRESIDENT OF THE BOARD OF DIRECTORS OF OBORO GALLERY IN MONTREAL.

DATE DUE

NOV 2 6 1985   NOV 26 1987

S. & W.   PAID NOR

DEC 3 1985

DEC 08 1987

MAY 0 1 1987   JAN 2 3 1989

MAR 3 0 1987   JAN 2 4 1989

APR 1 4 1987   FEB - 7 1989

APR 0 1   PAID NOR

OCT 3 1 1987   FEB 0 7 1989

OCT 2 9 1987   FEB 2 3 1989

NOV 1 2 1987
NOV 1 2 1987   FEB 2 2 1989

JAN 0 8 1990   JAN 3 - 1990